How Far Are You Willing To Go?
Murder Is Just The Beginning
(Rated PG) Part 2

How Far Are You Willing To Go?
Murder Is Just the Beginning
(Rated PG) Part 2

BY

TRACY WILSON

http://beautifulpublications.com

Published by
Beautiful Publications LLC
Stratford, CT 06614

PRINT ISBN: 978-0-9985765-1-0
EBOOK ISBN: 978-0-9985765-4-1

Printed in the United States of America

Dedication

This series is dedicated to my granddaughter, Shaliyah.

Chapter 54

"Trenice?"

"Yes Grandma?"

"You up yet?"

"I am now," I yawned.

"Vanessa's on the phone," she said as she closed the door to my room and went down the hall towards the kitchen.

"Hi Vanessa!" I exclaimed as Grandma put a cup of coffee in front of me on the table and sat down next to me.

"Hi Trenice... I'm afraid I have some bad news..."

"What's wrong?"

"The owner listed the property with Foxtons at the same time he listed with Weichert."

"Oh... so what does that mean?"

"I know you made an offer but someone else outbid you and the owner accepted their offer. I'm sorry Trenice."

"No need to be sorry Vanessa — We'll just make another offer..."

"Are you sure Trenice? This condo was pricey to begin with..."

"I thought you knew me Vanessa," I laughed.

"I just don't want you to get into a situation you can't handle Trenice."

"I know — and I appreciate it — but I want this condo."

"Sigh... ok Trenice... here goes... if you're willing to go as high as $330..."

"$330? What happened to $321?"

"You offered his asking price of $321 but you were outbid. The other offer was for $325."

"Well it doesn't make any sense for me to offer $330 then," I laughed.

"I'm really sorry about this Trenice — but I promise you I won't quit until we find you the home of your dreams."

"You already have," I laughed again.

"Come again?"

"Tell him we'll give him $350."

"What?"

"I said tell him we'll give him $350."

"Are you sure Trenice?"

"I'm sure."

"Ok Trenice — I'll get right on it — good luck."

"Thank you Vanessa."

"$350 huh?" Grandma asked as she brought me a second cup of coffee.

"Huh?" I asked as she interrupted my thoughts...

"This must be some place," she said as she placed two plates of scrambled eggs with cheese, home fries, sausage, and biscuits on the table and sat down next to me.

"It is Grandma," I said as I pulled the flyer out of my bathrobe pocket, passed it to her, and began dialing Jordan at work.

"Wow – this is beautiful – now I see why you're willing to make an offer of $350 – but where are you gettin' that kind of money?"

"Hello," Jordan said just in time.

"Hi honey."

"Hey Beautiful! You here from Vanessa yet?"

"Yea – that's why I'm callin' you..."

"What she say?"

"Someone else made an offer of $325 so I told her we'd offer $350."

"What are you nuts?"

"Yea...," I sighed.

"Trenice that'll take most of our money."

"I know."

"Are you sure?"

"I'm sure."

"Okay... keep me posted."

"I will honey."

"I love you."

"I love you too."

"Trenice?"

"Yes Grandma," I answered as I deliberately started eating the food she put in front of me.

"Where the hell are you gonna get $350 thousand dollars?"

"I'm not," I said as I finished the food and moved on to the second cup of coffee.

"How the hell are you gonna pay $350 thousand for a condo if you don't have $350 thousand dollars?"

"Hello?" I said as the phone rang just in time.

"Hi Trenice – the son-of-a-bitch got an offer for $375."

"Tell him we'll give him $400," I said as I swallowed my last bit of coffee."

"Are you sure Trenice?"

"Vanessa?"

"Ok, ok, ok – I'll get right on it," she said as Grandma started choking...

"Thanks Vanessa," I said as I started patting Grandma on her back...

"Whew that was rough," Grandma said.

"You ok Grandma?"

"I'm fine Trenice – are **YOU** ok?"

"Of course Grandma – why do you ask?"

"Well you said you don't have $350 thousand dollars and you tell the woman you'll pay $400 thousand dollars for this condo – what the hell is going on Trenice?"

"Grandma I'm just fine," I said as I kissed her forehead. "I'm gonna go jump in the shower and get dressed real quick before Vanessa calls back," I said as I ran down the hall and jumped in the shower before she had a chance to ask me anymore questions. When I got out the shower naturally, as luck would have it, I saw Aunt Trudy sitting at the kitchen table with Grandma.

"Hi Trenice," she said as I headed towards my room.

"Hi Aunt Trudy," I said as I made a beeline into the room and closed the door. As soon as I opened the door again, there she was ready to pounce...

"Ma showed me the flyer to the condo you want," she said.

"Oh ok," I said as I stood in the living room fixing my hair.

"It's really nice too – one of the doctors that works for the hospital lives in Hillcroft Towers..."

"Does he really? What's his name?" I asked, pretending to care...

"His name is Dr. Aiden."

"Oh ok – maybe I'll run into him if we get the place..."

"I'm surprised you can afford it – Ma told me you made an offer of $400 thousand dollars..."

"Yea... well I gotta run – by Grandma," I said as I kissed Grandma on the cheek and headed out the door as fast as I could.

"Something wrong with that girl," I heard Grandma say as I headed down the hallway. I just shook my head and made a beeline to my mother's house.

"Ma? Ma?"

"Who is it?"

"It's me!"

"Who the hell is me?"

"Trenice!"

"Then say that dammit!" she laughed as she opened the door and I ran inside. "What's your hurry?" she laughed as I ran past her.

"I gotta pee," I said as I ran towards the bathroom.

"Ma ain't got a bathroom?"

"Oh shut up Ma," I laughed as I came out the bathroom and sat down on the sofa.

"So you hear from Vanessa?"

"Yea."

"What she say?"

"She said he got another offer for $325, I offered $350, he got another offer for $375, so I offered $400."

"Trenice you feelin' alright?"

"Yes Ma," I laughed.

"I know you have some money but I know damn well you don't have $400 thousand dollars..."

"Okay."

"Okay? Is that all you have to say?"

"Yup."

"Okay – so what are you gonna do if he gets an offer for $425 or $450?"

"He won't Ma don't worry."

"You're the one that needs to be worried Trenice," she laughed.

"Hello?" I answered as the phone rang.

"Hey Beautiful," Jordan said.

"Hi Honey. How'd you know I was here?"

"You're grandmother told me to try you here."

"Oh ok."

"So you hear from Vanessa yet?"

"Yea – she said the son-of-a-bitch got an offer for $375 so I told her we'd offer $400."

"Trenice are you crazy???"

"Nope."

"Why in the world would you tell her $400? We can't afford that."

"Yes we can."

"Trenice, we don't have $400 in the bank. The only way we can afford.... ooohhh..... ok... now I know what you're up to," he laughed.

"I knew you'd figure it out," I laughed.

"We'll see if he accepts the offer of $400 – I mean when – the only way we won't get this condo is if he gets a higher offer – then we'll talk about how much we wana put down and we'll get a small mortgage if we have to – I was hoping we wouldn't have to get a mortgage at all but from the figures you printed from the mortgage calculator yesterday we can handle a $50,000 mortgage if necessary."

"I know," I laughed.

"Well call me back and let me know what she says – I gotta get back out front – I love you."

"I love you too – I'll talk to you later," I said as we both hung up.

"Hello?" I answered as I snatched the phone up again.

"May I speak to Trenice please?"

"Hi Vanessa."

"Oh hi Trenice – I'm glad I caught you."

"Wow – that was quick."

"Well you offered $400 right?"

"Yes."

"Well we left off at the other offer of $375 and I was just about to call him and tell him you were willing to offer $400 but before I could call him he called me..."

"He did?"

"Yes – and guess what Trenice?"

"What?"

"The bank wouldn't approve the mortgage for $375 for the person that outbid you – so the owner is willing to accept your bid of $350!"

"Oh my God, oh my God, oh my God!" I screamed.

"I take it that's a yes!" she yelled.

"Yes! Yes! Yes!" I screamed.

"What the hell is going on?" my mother interrupted.

"We got the condo!" I screamed as I dropped the phone and my mother and I started jumping up and down...

"HEEELLLOOO?"

"Oh - sorry Vanessa," I laughed.

"I'll get right on this – but I need to ask you – is there any chance you won't get approved for a mortgage Trenice?"

"We don't need one."

"Come again?"

"We don't need one," I repeated.

"Oooohhkkaaay! I'll get back to you before the end of this week – congratulations on your new home Trenice!"

"Thank you Vanessa," I said as I hung up the phone.

"Trenice you are too much," my mother laughed.

"Do I remind you of anyone you know?" I laughed.

"Girl I'm so happy for you – where's the flyer so we can show April and June?"

"Oh I left it at Grandma's house."

"Oh boy – I know she had a bunch of questions didn't she?"

"Not really – she just asked me was I feelin' alright 'cause I offered $400 when I didn't even have $350," I laughed.

"I'm surprised she didn't push you for an explanation," she laughed.

"I'm surprised Aunt Trudy didn't push me for an explanation," I laughed.

"Trudy saw the flyer? And she didn't ask you how you were payin' for it?"

"Not exactly – she just said she's surprised I can afford it," I laughed.

"Damn you got off easy," she laughed.

"I told them I had to run – then I ran," I said as we laughed so hard we were holding our stomachs.

"Well you gettin' it for $350 - $50 thousand less than you offered but $29 thousand more than the asking price."

"It's so beautiful Ma. It's worth every penny."

"Yes it is Trenice. You and Jordan will be very happy there."

"Oh my God – I forgot just that quick," I laughed as I picked up the phone…"

"Girl you have to deliver this news in person," she said as she snatched the phone out of my hand, pulled me up off the sofa, and we headed out the door.

"Hi honey!" I yelled down the corridor as soon as we got there…

"Hey Beautiful! Be right with ya," he said as he finished with his customer and came down the corridor towards us. "Hello Miss Claire," he said as he pulled me into a hug.

"You goin' to lunch Jordan?" his supervisor yelled down the corridor.

"Naaa... I'm gone for the day – see y'all tomorrow," he said as we left the store.

"You already know don't you?" my mother asked.

"I do now," he laughed.

"We did it honey!" I squealed.

"We did it!" Jordan squealed as he picked us both up off the ground.

"Jordan put me down," my mother laughed.

"I'm so happy – after Trenice told me we offered $400 I pretty much gave up hope," he said.

"Why Jordan?" my mother asked.

"Well the way the bids were goin' I just knew we'd be outbid again," he said.

"I'm surprised you weren't," my mother said.

"God was with us," I said.

"What happened Trenice?" my mother asked.

"Well remember when I made the offer of $400?"

"Yes," they both said in unison.

"Well Vanessa called me at mom's house and she said just as she was about to call and make the counter offer the owner called her to tell her the bank didn't approve the mortgage of $375 for the person that outbid us – so he wanted to let her know that he was accepting our offer of $350!" I screamed.

"You mean she never got the chance to tell him we made an offer of $400?" Jordan asked.

"Yes! He told her he'd accept our offer of $350 before she got a chance to say anything at all!"

"God is definitely looking out for you two," my mother said.

"And the best part of this is we won't have a mortgage at all!" I yelled.

"You won't have a mortgage Trenice?"

"Nope."

"I knew you had the money," my mother laughed.

"Yup," I laughed.

"This way ladies," Jordan said as he escorted us to the car.

"Where we off too Jordan?" my mother asked.

"You'll see," Jordan said as we drove off.

Chapter 55

"Well, well – this is a pleasant surprise!" Jake said as he came downstairs to greet us. "What's the occasion?" he asked as my mother got out the car.

"I'll let them tell ya," my mother said as she stretched and yawned.

"Hello Miss Claire," Rachel said when she got downstairs. "Hi Jordan, Hi Trenice – what's going on?"

"We did it!" Jordan and I said in unison.

"Y'all got married?" Rachel asked.

"Not yet," we said in unison.

"Oh boy – honey they're already starting that - it's just a matter of time," Rachel laughed.

"Well what **DID** you do?" Jake asked.

"We bought a condo," Jordan said.

"Damn that was fast – it usually takes a while before you find what you want…"

"I thought you knew my daughter better than that," my mother laughed.

"Yea Rachel – I thought you knew Trenice better than that," Jake laughed.

"Well where is it?" Rachel asked.

"600 North Broadway," my mother answered matter-of-factly.

"Oh my God!   Those condos are beautiful! How'd you manage that?"

"Well Rachel, I got tired of waiting for Vanessa to call me back so I started looking on my own – I found it online yesterday, we went to see it last night, and we made the offer today," I said.

"Wow – I'm surprised you can afford it – I know there's a waiting list a mile long to get in there," she laughed.

"Well Rachel, you're not alone – my mother was surprised along with my Aunt Trudy - and my grandmother thinks there's something wrong with me," I laughed.

"Aside from the fact that you need to get the hell out of her house, ain't a damn thing wrong with you," she laughed.

"Well it's about time – especially after what happened last week," my mother laughed.

"What happened?" Jake asked.

"Long story," Jordan laughed.

"We got plenty of time – Jake can make us drinks and you can both tell us all about it," Rachel laughed as we followed her upstairs.

"Oh boy – I gotta hear this one," Jake laughed as we all went inside.

"Trenice, what's Char's number?" Rachel asked.

"963-1323," I said. "Why?"

"Char?" Rachel asked as I listened to her side of the phone conversation... "Yea – she's here.... uhuh... yea – Miss Claire's here too... uhuh... well the reason I called you is 'cause they found a place so we need to plan the housewarming... uhuh... I know you're taking care of that but... yea... ok – see you in about 5 minutes."

"I take back what I said earlier Rachel – you do know Trenice after all," my mother laughed.

"I sure do," she laughed.

"You gave Char a list already?" my mother asked.

"Yea Ma – she's on it," I laughed.

"You told her I was making baked macaroni & cheese?"

"I told her I didn't care – they could bring as much as they want," I laughed.

"That's all well and good Trenice but I know you want more than macaroni & cheese," my mother laughed.

"What do you want us to bring Trenice?" Jake asked as he gave us our drinks.

"Aww shit... maybe we should ask Jake to be the bartender," my mother laughed after she took a sip of her drink.

"Oh that's right - you never had one of Jake's drinks," Rachel laughed. "Good isn't it?"

"Oh yeaaaa," my mother slurred as she continued sipping her drink and we all bust out laughing.

"What's so funny?" Char asked as she came into the living room with us.

"Hi Char!" we all said in unison.

"Hi everybody!" she said as she sat down, holding out her hand. We all bust out laughing again.

"Coming right up maam," Jake said as he handed Char her drink and sat down with us.

"I now officially call this meeting to order – now let's get down to business," Rachel said.

"Yes maam!" we all said in unison.

"Trenice, how soon do you think they'll be moved in?"

"I think we can close in about a week," I laughed.

"Trenice, you need time to get a mortgage – then you have to deal with all the paperwork at the bank – credit scores... you can't do all that in a week," Char laughed.

"You're right – that's why I'm glad we don't have to," I said.

"You don't have to? How the hell can you buy a condo and close in a week without dealing with the bank?" she asked.

"We have the money," I said.

"**WHAT?**" Jake, Rachel, and Char yelled in unison.

"We have the money," I repeated.

"Where the hell... oh... never mind," Char laughed.

"**OH!**" Jake and Rachel yelled in unison.

"Yeaaa... they know you pretty well I see," my mother laughed.

"Well let's get back to the business at hand," Rachel said.

"Okay then," I said as I picked up the phone and called Vanessa. "Hi Vanessa.... uhuh... oh you did? Oh he did? We can close on Friday? I'm soooo excited... me too... ok then... me too... see you Friday afternoon... thank you soooo much for everything Vanessa.... bye."

"What'd she say?" Jordan asked.

"She said the seller wants to do this as quickly as possible. She spoke to Tyler and faxed him a copy of the papers. We have an appointment in Tyler's office on Friday at 3pm – after we sign everything and give them a certified check, we get the keys!"

"So we can do your housewarming on Saturday then?" Rachel asked.

"Yea," Jordan said.

"Ok so what are we bringing?" Jake asked.

"I'm bringing baked macaroni & cheese!" my mother yelled.

"We hear you Miss Claire," Char laughed as she wrote it down.

"We'll bring lasagna," Jake said.

"Got it," Char said as she wrote it down.

"So what's your new home look like?" Rachel asked.

"Hang on a second," I said as I pulled it up on her computer and printed out the flyer.

"Oh Trenice – it's beautiful!" Rachel said.

"Congrats," Jake said as he looked at the flyer.

"Thank you, thank you," Jordan said as he finished his drink.

"Ok – Char do you have the names of everyone Trenice wants to invite?" Rachel asked.

"Yea," she said as she handed Rachel the list.

"Great – All I have to do is put the names on the invitations and fill in the date – makes my job easier," Rachel laughed.

16

"You already have the invitations?" my mother asked.

"You know how Trenice is – you gotta stay two steps ahead of her," Rachel laughed.

"Well how will we know who's bringing what?" Char asked.

"We won't," Rachel said.

"So what if we get 8 tons of macaroni & cheese then?" my mother asked.

"Trenice better have a lot of toilet paper," she said as we all bust out laughing.

"I wouldn't worry about it hon – we'll get a nice variety – besides, pasta n liquor go down good," Jake said as we all bust out laughing again.

"Well we know you'll have something to sit on 'cause I'm buying you that sectional," my mother laughed.

"And we'll have something to sleep on too 'cause Mum-Mum already told us they knew the perfect gift to get us – a king-sized bed with a steel frame so we can't break it," Jordan said as everyone bust out laughing.

"Oh boy – I know just what to get you now," Char laughed.

"So do we," Jake laughed.

Sounds good – I guess you'll see everything else when you get it," Rachel said as she and Char compared lists.

"Okay then... now that that's all settled... what the hell happened last week Trenice?" Rachel asked.

"Girl, you ain't tell them what happened last week?" my mother asked.

"Not yet," I laughed.

"Oh boy – Trudy right?" Char asked.

"Girl you don't know the half of it," my mother laughed.

"Well I'd like to," Rachel said.

"Y'all remember when I was with Torbett?" I asked.

"Yea," Char said.

"Jake and Rachel didn't know me then," I said.

"Torbett was your ex?" Jake asked.

"Yea," I answered.

"Oh ok – so what happened?"

"Well, to make a long story short..."

"Who said you gotta make a long story short?" Rachel asked.

"Aiight, aiight," I laughed. "Anyway, I was in love with Torbett since high school and one night he came over to surprise me with an engagement ring," I said.

"Le'me find out Trenice was gonna marry another man," Jake laughed.

"So he asked me to marry him and I said yes," I said as I finished my drink.

"So when we came upstairs we threw his ass out before he got a chance to tell us he asked Trenice to marry him and she said yes," my mother said.

"Then damn!" Char said.

"Trenice why didn't you just tell your mother what he was doing in the house?" Jake asked.

"I didn't get a chance to – all hell broke loose – so I went straight to grandma's house and I've been there ever since."

"Oh so that's why you live with your grandmother," Rachel said.

"That's only part of it Rachel. Trenice was hurt and she also knew I didn't really like Torbett to begin with so she figured there was no point in telling me," my mother said.

"Well I would'a told you," Rachel said.

"Rachel shut the hell up – when you threw up all over your mother's butter leather couch and she told you get the fuck outta her house you ain't tell your mother shit," Jake laughed.

"That was different," she laughed.

"Well Trenice didn't tell me but she did tell her grandmother and Trudy – and they never told me."

"Trenice how long ago was this?" Rachel asked.

"About 3 years ago," I said.

"3 years? And they never told your mother what happened?"

"Nope."

"And here's the kicker – Trenice thought I knew all along and didn't give a damn," my mother said.

"Then damn!" Char said.

"Unfuckin' believable," Rachel said.

"Well I went over there and I lit into their asses," my mother said.

"What'd you do Miss Claire?" Char asked.

"I told Ma and Trudy they knew damn well they should'a told me – of course they both said I was just mad 'cause they knew and I didn't – which I was – but anyway – the shit hit the fan when Sissy got in my face and I choked the shit outta her…"

THEN DAMN!" Char yelled.

"Miss Claire you didn't!" Jake said.

"Oh yes the hell she did," Jordan laughed. "We were in the hallway listenin' and crackin' up – Miss

Claire told Sissy she wasn't Trenice and she'd bust her fuckin' ass!" Jordan laughed.

"I hear ya Miss Claire," Rachel laughed.

"Yea well she didn't hear me 'cause she had the nerve to tell me she wasn't gonna let me sit there and disrespect 'Miss Gladys' as she put it – so I said didn't I tell you to mind your business bitch – and I started chokin' the shit outta her," my mother laughed.

"So you n Trenice listenin' in the hallway crackin' up while your mother's chokin' the shit outta her," Jake said to us.

"Yea – we probably woulda stayed in the hallway but once Trudy got on her mother Trenice made a beeline in the house, pulled Trudy by the back of her shirt, and told her get the fuck off her mother," Jordan laughed.

"I hear that girl!" Char and Rachel said as we high-fived.

"It was on after Trudy knocked Trenice on the floor though," Jordan laughed.

"She hurt you Trenice?" Rachel asked.

"Naa... but Grandma was about to hurt us," I laughed.

"Whatchu mean?" Char asked.

"Oh nothing – she just got her gun out the kitchen drawer and fired it," my mother laughed.

"**WHAT?**" Char, Jake, and Rachel yelled in unison.

"Stopped everyone in their tracks too," my mother laughed.

"How long Miss Gladys been packin'" Rachel asked.

"Ever since she worked at the Black Horse," I laughed.

"She went down the hall towards her room but when Trudy started her shit she came right back down the hall again with the gun in her hand," Jordan laughed.

"I don't believe this shit," Jake laughed.

"I ain't never seen no shit like that in my life," Jordan laughed.

"Yea – Sissy said she was leavin' so Jordan was only too happy to hold the door open for her – so Trudy gonna say oh I know you ain't throwin' nobody out my mother's house," my mother laughed.

"Yea – so Trenice said bitch please – Trudy told her shut the fuck up, and here come Miss Gladys again talkin' about she still got people that wanna act a fool up in her house," Jordan laughed.

"Oh my God – I would'a laughed all in that bitch's face," Char laughed.

"Oh we did – when we left," Jordan said.

"You mean you stayed there after that?" Rachel laughed.

"Hell yea – Jordan asked Ma if she was shootin' blanks and Ma asked him if he ever played Russian Roulette," my mother laughed.

"AAAWWWW SHIT!!!" Char, Jake, and Rachel all yelled in unison.

"The best part was when Ma started tellin' us about when she caught Trudy's boyfriend in her room and she pulled the gun on him," my mother laughed.

"Get the fuck outta here!" Jake yelled.

"Ma didn't play that shit – she told him if she ever caught him in the house again she'd blow his head off," my mother hollered.

"Yea – she said he ran out the house with his pants in his hand," Jordan laughed.

"Once we got outside and saw them sittin' on the bench I couldn't help but bust out laughin' and didn't give a damn who didn't like it," my mother laughed.

"Wooooee," Rachel laughed with tears in her eyes. "I'da been cryin'" she laughed.

"I'da laughed all up in the bitch's face," Char said.

"Oh we did," Jordan laughed.

"Yea – it's about time you get the fuck outta her house now," Jake laughed.

"Yes it is – in fact she kinda told me that earlier today," I laughed.

"You lyin!" Char said.

"Well she didn't exactly say that but she did tell me if I'd stop printin' out my emails and go pick up the damn phone I just might get outta her house sooner," I laughed.

"Damn Trenice – she's really mad huh?" Rachel asked.

"Ma just has a bug up her ass – she'll get over it," my mother laughed.

"Miss Claire you are too much," Rachel laughed.

"You spend a little more time with us you'll know," my mother laughed.

"We better keep our distance until Jordan and Trenice move out," Jake laughed.

"Oh please – Miss Glady's 'll be right there helpin' Trenice pack, shoppin' for her house – she ain't gonna stay mad at Trenice – she can't stay mad at her baby," Char laughed.

"You right about that Char," my mother laughed.

"Well I gotta get goin' y'all – I gotta work tonight," Char said as she got up.

"We might as well get going too," I said as I got up. "Guess I gotta go pack now right honey?"

"Yea," Jordan said as he pulled me into a kiss.

"Well I'ma go too – nice seeing you again Jake, Rachel," my mother said as she got up.

"Nice seeing you again Miss Claire – we'll see you Saturday," Jake said as he walked us to the door.

"Bye y'all," Char said as she went downstairs.

"Bye everybody! See you Saturday!" Rachel said as we all left.

Chapter 56

"Hi Mum-Mum," Jordan said as Miss April opened the door and we went inside.

"Hi Miss April, Hi Miss June," I said as we sat down.

"Hey , hey," Miss June said.

"Hey, hey – where y'all been?" Miss April asked.

"We been hangin' out," my mother laughed.

"Oh? We celebratin' again?"

"Yea girl," my mother said as she showed her the flyer of the condo.

"Wow! This is beautiful!" Miss April said as she passed the flyer to Miss June.

"This is really beautiful," Miss June said.

"So this is where you were headed earlier?" Miss April asked.

"No – we went to see it yesterday – we just came from Jake & Rachel's," Jordan said.

"Claire you went with them?" Miss June asked.

"Yea – I went with them," she laughed.

"You tell them about what happened last week?" Miss April asked.

"Yea – but we had business to take care of 1st," my mother laughed.

"Business?" Miss June asked.

"Yea – Rachel called the meeting to order and we planned their housewarming," my mother said.

"Oh ok – so we gotta get that bed delivered by Saturday," Miss April laughed.

"I heard about that," my mother laughed.

"Oh you did did ya?" Miss June laughed.

"I sure did – Jordan told me after I said I was buyin' the sectional," she laughed.

"Well we know they'll have a place to sit and a place to sleep," Miss June laughed.

"They'll have more than that by the weekend," my mother laughed.

"Well let me say this – Jordan, Trenice – don't buy anything until after your housewarming," Miss April laughed.

"Oh we won't" Jordan laughed.

"So when do you close?" Miss June asked.

"We get the keys Friday afternoon," I said.

"Damn you move fast girl!" Miss April laughed.

"Reminds me of someone else I know," Miss June laughed.

"Oh shut up June," my mother laughed.

"Well at least we know where to have everything delivered," Miss April said.

"Yea – and they're having their housewarming in their house so you don't have to carry gifts from place to place – all you have to do is put the gifts away," my mother laughed.

"Yea and clean up," Jordan laughed.

"I'm so happy for you," Miss April said as she hugged us both.

"Le'me get in there," Miss June said as she joined in.

"Le'me get in there too," my mother said as she joined in the group hug.

"I'm happy for us too Beautiful," Jordan said as he pulled me into a kiss.

"AWWW...." they all said in unison.

"So you packin' like Glady's Trenice?" Miss April asked.

"Hell No!" I laughed.

"I could'a told ya that April – Trenice wouldn't even put Ma's gun away," my mother laughed.

"Was it loaded?" Miss June asked.

"No it wasn't – but Trenice wouldn't touch it," my mother laughed.

"Trenice you know damn well Gladys didn't have any bullets in it," Miss April laughed.

"She had somethin' in it when she fired it," I laughed.

"Claire! You didn't tell me she fired the damn thing," Miss June laughed.

"Yea she did – and she came back down the hall to fire it again when Trudy n Trenice started goin' at it again," my mother laughed.

"Claire she wasn't gonna do a damn thing but throw y'all out her house," Miss April laughed.

Tracy Wilson

"I know – but who's to say she wouldn't have gone upside somebody's head first?" my mother laughed.

"Yea – like mine," I laughed.

"Le'me tell you somethin' Trenice – if Gladys was goin' upside anybody's head – it was Trudy's – not yours," Miss April laughed.

"Damn right," Jordan said.

"Yea Trenice – Ma had no intention of doin' anything to you – ain't that much mad in the world," my mother laughed.

"Glad you think so," I said.

"Trust me Trenice – she might'a pushed ya but that's about it," Miss June laughed.

"You know you her baby – that's why Trudy always goin' at you the way she do," Miss April laughed.

"Well thank God it won't be for much longer," I said.

"How 'bout that?" my mother laughed.

"Especially since you're moving so far up North Broadway," Miss June said.

"My grandson is mooovin' on up with my new granddaughter-in-law," Miss April laughed.

"To the east side... to a deluxe condo in the skyyyyy," Miss June sang...

"Mooovin' on up... mooovin' on up... to the east side... mooovin' on up..." they all sang in unison...

"We finally got a piece of the pie!" Jordan and I sang...

"Fish don't fry in the kitchen..." Miss April sang..."

"Beans don't burn on the grill..." Miss June sang...

27

"Took a whole lot of trrrryyiiinn... just to get up the hill..." my mother sang...

"Now we're up in the big league... gettin, our turn at bat... as long as we live... it's you n me babyyy... and ain't nothin' wrong with that!" Jordan and I sang...

"Well we're mooovin' on up... mooovin' on up... to the east side... mooovin' on up..." we all sang in unison...

"To a deluxe condo in the skyyyyy," Miss June sang...

"Mooovin' on up... mooovin' on up... to the east side... mooovin' on up..." they all sang in unison...

"We finally got a piece of the piieee.... iiieee..." we all sang in unison as we high-fived and hugged.

Chapter 57

"Mornin' Grandma," I said as I went down the hall towards the kitchen.

"Mornin' Trenice," she said as she put 2 cups of coffee on the table. "Well, I guess this is it," she said as she sat down.

"Yea," I sighed.

"You don't have to be so happy about it," she laughed.

"I can't help it," I laughed.

"I know," she said. "I'm glad you're finally gonna be happy," she said as she sipped on her coffee.

"Me too Grandma – meeeee…. toooooo," I said as I sipped on my coffee.

"So when you leavin'," Aunt Trudy asked as she came in with Sissy.

"Good morning to you too," I said as I continued sipping my coffee.

"Don't start that shit you two," Grandma said.

"What?" Aunt Trudy asked.

"You leavin' Trenice?" Sissy asked.

"Yes Sissy," I said.

"When you leavin?" she asked.

"Why?" you helpin' me pack?" I laughed.

"Hell no," she laughed.

"Ma whatchu got to eat?" Aunt Trudy asked as she fumbled around in the kitchen...

"Whatever you find in there," Grandma said.

"I hear you movin' to 600 North Broadway," Sissy said.

"Yup," I said.

"Those condos are nice – I heard there's a waiting list to get in there," she said.

"Yup," I said.

"I'm surprised you can afford it," she said.

"You ain't the only one," I said with a smirk. Grandma didn't say anything but she rolled her eyes as we continued...

"So where you get the money for a condo up there?" she asked.

"Mind your fuckin' business Sissy!" I said as I continued sipping my coffee.

"Well!" she said.

"Why you gotta be so rude Trenice?" Aunt Trudy asked.

"Rude? How am I being rude?"

"She just asked you a question."

"And I just answered her."

"You just don't want nobody to know y'all got money," she said.

"Whatever," I said as I finished my coffee and got up from the table. "I gotta get goin' – see you later

Grandma," I said as I left. I stayed at my mother's house until Jordan came to pick me up...

"You ready to go get the keys to our new home Beautiful?" he said as he pulled me into a deep kiss.

"Hell yea!" I said as I kissed him back.

"I guess I'll see you tomorrow," my mother laughed.

"See you tomorrow Ma," I yelled out the window as we pulled off. You would think it was 5:00 already with all the traffic we hit on 287 but we finally made it to Tyler's office...

"Hi Jordan, Hi Trenice – congratulations," the receptionist said as we walked in.

"Thank you, thank you," I said.

"They're waiting for you in conference room 1, she said as we headed down the hall and went inside.

"Hi Jordan, Hi Trenice – a pleasure to see you again," Tyler said as we shook his hand.

"Hi Tyler, Hi Vanessa," Jordan said as he sat down.

"Hi Vanessa, I said as I sat down.

"Hi Jordan, Hi Trenice. Do you have any other questions before we get started?"

"Nope!" we said in unison.

"I looked over the papers – everything is in order – just sign where Vanessa's indicated with the x's, give her the certified checks, and you can get the keys," Tyler said.

"Sounds good to us," Jordan said.

"What name is going on the title?" Vanessa asked.

"Both our names," I said.

"Both our names?" Jordan asked.

"Yea," I said.

"Alrighty then!" Jordan said as we started to sign the papers. Tyler and Vanessa waited for another 20 minutes or so for us to finishing signing all 14 pages.

"Checks please," Vanessa laughed.

"Here you go," I said as I handed them to her.

"Welcome to your new home!" she said as she handed each of us a set of keys.

"Our new home!" we said in unison.

"This calls for a toast!" Tyler said as he opened a bottle of champagne and poured each of us a glass...

"None for me – I'm driving," Jordan laughed.

"Aww cmon honey – just one sip," I said.

"Ok Beautiful," he said as he raised his glass along with the rest of us.

"To beautiful beginnings," Tyler said as he took a sip of champagne.

"To beautiful beginnings," we repeated as we took a sip of champagne.

"To a happy home," Vanessa said as she took a sip of champagne.

"To a happy home," we repeated as we took another sip of champagne.

"That's it for me – I gotta drive," Jordan said as he put down his glass. "Hate to see good champagne go to waste," he said as he went to pour it out...

"Who said anything about good champagne going to waste? I ain't driving!" I laughed as I snatched his glass from him, drank his champagne, and then finished mine. Tyler and Vanessa bust out laughing.

"Here's the rest," Tyler laughed as he handed me the bottle of champagne. "Congrats again."

"Thank you Tyler," I said as I gave him a hug.

"Thanks for everything," Jordan said as they shook hands.

"Thanks for everything Vanessa," I said as I gave her a hug.

"Thanks Vanessa," Jordan said as he gave her a hug.

"You're welcome – and thank you!" she said as we all went towards the lobby.

"Congrats Jordan, congrats Trenice!" the receptionist said as we left Tyler's office and went into the elevator.

"Let's go home..." I sighed as I leaned into Jordan.

"Let's go home..." he said as we got off the elevator and left the building. We didn't say anything for the entire ride back to Yonkers. We didn't even complain about hitting more traffic on 287. We could've been stuck in a blizzard and it wouldn't have made a difference. We went to Jordan's house first...

"Ok Mum-Mum – this is it," Jordan said as he brought down the last box. When he came back upstairs it was all hugs and kisses...

"Take care... we love you," Miss April said.

"We love you too," Jordan said.

"Oh stop it Ma – they only movin' up North Broadway – we gonna see 'em tomorrow," Miss June laughed.

"Oh shut up," Miss April said as she wiped the tears from her eyes and we went downstairs.

"Almost there Beautiful," Jordan said as we headed up North Broadway.

"Almost there," I said as we pulled up in front of grandma's house.

"They here Ma," Aunt Trudy said as we came in.

"You sure you got everything Trenice?" Grandma asked as Jordan started taking the boxes downstairs.

"I'm sure Grandma," I said as I went down the hall to my empty room and looked at it one last time.

"Whatcha doin?" Grandma asked as she came up behind me.

"Nuthin...," I sighed as I kept looking in my empty room.

"You okay Trenice?" she asked.

"Yea..." I sighed.

"Well c'mon – don't keep the man waitin', she said as we went back down the hall.

"So you're finally leavin'," Sissy said.

"Yea...," I sighed.

"Well I hope you're happy!" she snapped sarcastically.

"Oh we are – trust me," Jordan said as he came up behind me and pulled me close to him.

"Congratulations – I won't be able to come to your housewarming tomorrow 'cause I gotta work – but I'ma send your gift with Ma," Aunt Trudy said.

"Thank you Aunt Trudy," I said.

"Oh well – might as well get goin'," Grandma said as she pulled us into hugs and kisses...

"Ok Grandma," I laughed as she squeezed me so hard I couldn't breathe...

"Jordan you take care of her or you'll answer to me," she said.

"Oh I know," Jordan laughed.

"I love you Trenice," Grandma said as she squeezed me.

"I love you too Grandma," I said as I squeezed her back.

"You sure you don't wanna take your bed so you'll have somethin' to sleep on tonight?" she asked.

"Naa... we'll sleep on the floor," I said.

"Sleep on the floor? You got sleepin' bags or somethin'?" Sissy asked.

"Nope," Jordan said.

"Shiiiitttt – if I were you I'd take the damn bed – hell if I'd sleep on the damn floor," she laughed.

"Alright Miss Gladys, Trudy, Sissy – we gotta get goin' – see you tomorrow," Jordan said as we headed towards the door.

"See you tomorrow Trenice," Grandma said.

"See you tomorrow Grandma," I said as we went downstairs.

"Almost there Beautiful," Jordan said as we got in the car.

"Almost there," I said as we headed up North Broadway. When we got there Carl was waiting for us...

"Evening Jordan, Evening Trenice – let me get these for you," he said as he put all our things on the luggage cart and wheeled them into the lobby to the elevator for us. "You can go on upstairs if you like – I'll have the car parked for you and I'll bring you your keys when I bring your things up," Carl said.

"Thanks Carl," Jordan said as we went into the elevator. We didn't say anything until we got to our front door.

"We're home Beautiful!" Jordan yelled as he picked me up in his arms...

"Were home!" I yelled as I opened the door and he carried me inside.

"Home...," Jordan said as he started kissing me slowly and passionately...

"Home...," I whispered as I kissed him back.

"Who is it?" Jordan asked, slightly annoyed that we had been interrupted.

"Carl."

"Hi Carl," I said as Jordan opened the door.

"Where would you like me to put your things?"

"Oh we'll take care of it," Jordan said.

"I insist," Carl said.

"Ok then – the master bedroom is at the end of the hall and this bedroom will be the office," Jordan said as he showed Carl where to put our things. It didn't take him long.

"Good night," Carl said as he started to leave.

"Good night Carl," Jordan said as he slipped him a tip.

"Thank you," Carl said as he left.

"Now... where were we?" Jordan whispered as he took me by the hand, led me into the bedroom, and laid me down on the floor...

"Home...," I said as he started kissing me slowly and passionately again...

"Home...," he said as we continued kissing until we fell asleep.

Chapter 58

The morning started out with a bang – literally.

"Jordan! Trenice! Will y'all get up and answer the damn door already?" he yelled as he continued to bang on the door...

"Honey... get the door..." I yawned as I pulled myself up onto my knees and stood up.

"Oh I'll get it alright," Jordan growled as he jumped and started down the hall... "I don't give a damn who it is – mothafucka bangin' on my damn door at 8:30 Saturday mornin' talkin' 'bout get up and answer the damn door... who the fuck he think he talkin' to?" Jordan continued to growl as he snatched the door open... "Carl, let me tell you one fuckin' thing right now..."

"You see all this?" Carl interrupted as he pointed down the hall.

"'Mornin' Carl, I yawned as I poked my head between them and looked down the hall at all the boxes.

"Yea I see it – so what?" Jordan growled.

"It's all for you – I been standin' here bangin' on your door for about 20 minutes – they threatenin' to take the shit back – y'all had to answer the damn door 'cause I wasn't takin' shit back downstairs," he laughed.

"Aiight man you got that – good lookin'," Jordan said as he went to take one of the boxes.

"Excuse me sir," the deliveryman said.

"Yea?" Jordan asked.

"We were given explicit instructions that you were not to touch these boxes," he said.

"Fine," Jordan growled. "But if we don't touch them, how the hell we supposed to get them in the house?" Jordan asked with his arms folded.

"We've been instructed to do that for you sir," he said.

"Where you from man?" Jordan asked.

"Raymour & Flanigan," he said.

"Furniture?" Jordan asked.

"Yes sir," he answered.

"Trenice – get outta their way," Jordan laughed as he opened the door for them.

"Well I guess I can go back downstairs and tell the other guys to bring up the rest now," Carl laughed.

"The rest?" We said in unison.

"You haven't seen half of it," Carl laughed as he headed toward the elevator with the deliveryman.

"Might as well put on a pot of coffee," I yawned as I headed towards the kitchen.

"Good idea," Jordan laughed as he opened the door and Carl escorted 3 delivery men in.

"Sir, where would you like us to put your dinning set?" I asked as I came into the living room…

"Follow me," I said.

"Yes maam," the 1st delivery man answered.

"Honey look!" I said as I handed Jordan the attached card.

"Enjoy! Love Char," Jordan read.

"Awww… that's really sweet – but we have a lot of things to bring upstairs for you so if you'll just show us where to put this maam…"

"Right this way," Jordan said as he put the card in his bathrobe pocket and escorted the deliverymen to the dining room.

"Jordan I'ma go back downstairs to the lobby – call me if you need anything," Carl said as he left.

"Coffee sure smells good," the 2nd deliveryman said.

"It's hazelnut," I said as I continued sipping on my coffee.

"Aiight John – let's go get the rest," the 1st deliveryman said as they all went back into the hallway to get more boxes.

"Sir, where would you like us to put your entertainment unit?" the 1st deliveryman asked.

"C'mere Beautiful," Jordan said as I came into the living room and handed Jordan the attached card.

"For future entertainment! Love Jake & Rachel," Jordan read.

"You can put this right on that wall," I said pointing to the left.

"Yes maam," John said.

"We'll be right back," the 1ˢᵗ deliveryman said as they went back into the hallway and Jordan put the card in his bathrobe pocket.

"I don't believe this," Jordan said as they came back.

"Play nice and don't break it! Love Mum-mum," I laughed as I read it.

"Where to?" the 1ˢᵗ deliveryman asked.

"Right this way," Jordan said as he put the card in his bathrobe pocket and took them down the hall to the master bedroom.

"We'll be right back with your mattress and box spring," John said as they went out into the hall.

"Wow!" I said when they came back in and headed down towards the master bedroom with the mattress and box spring.

"We'll need to go downstairs and get the rest of the furniture off the truck – we'll be gone for a few minutes 'cause we need to unload the furniture, put it on the elevator, then put it in the hallway," the 1ˢᵗ deliveryman said as they left.

"I hope you made plenty of coffee," Jordan laughed.

"I did – it's the least we can do for them – I'm gonna go whip up some breakfast for them too," I laughed.

"We'll be eating a lot today – don't make too much," he laughed.

"Oh I won't – just some scrambled eggs, sausage, and biscuits," I laughed.

"That sounds good – they'll appreciate it and so will I," he laughed.

"Comin' right up honey," I laughed as I went into the kitchen and finished breakfast. Fortunately for us the sausage and biscuits were already done 'cause Jordan needed me again...

"Beautiful you are not going to believe this," he said as I came back out into the living room...

"Oh my God!" I said as I read the card. "For your new home! Love Grandma," I read.

"This set won't fit in your bedroom with the other one," the 1st deliveryman said.

"Right this way gentelemen," Jordan said as he put the card in his bathrobe pocket and they followed him to the 2nd bedroom.

"We'll be right back with your mattress and box spring," John said as they went out into the hall.

"They thought of everything didn't they Beautiful?" Jordan said as he pulled me into a kiss.

"They sure did," I said as I kissed him back.

"Excuse us," the 1st deliveryman said as they came back in and headed down the hall with the 2nd mattress and box spring.

"Almost done," the 1st deliveryman said as they headed out into the hallway to get the rest of the boxes.

"We'll start setting up your furniture as soon as we get this outta these boxes," John said as they started to tear open the 1st box...

"Wait!" I yelled.

"Something wrong maam?" the 1st deliveryman asked.

"Yes." I said.

"What's the problem maam?" he asked.

"We wanna read the card first," I laughed.

"Enjoy! Love Ma," Jordan read.

"You sure have nice parents," the 1st deliveryman said.

"Shit – I wish I had parents like theirs," John laughed.

"Can we start setting up now maam?" the 1st deliveryman asked.

"Sure," I said as Jordan put the card in his bathrobe pocket and they started tearing open the boxes.

"Oh my God – it's beautiful!" I said as they set up the sectional.

"It looks really good in here with the entertainment center too – your mother was right Beautiful," Jordan said as he pulled me into a kiss.

"She sure was," I said as I kissed him back. The deliverymen continued setting up the sectional and moved on to the entertainment center as if we weren't standing in the middle of the floor.

"I'll be right back," I said as I went into the kitchen and came back with 2 plates of food.

"Thanks Beautiful, Jordan said as he started eating.

"Thanks Beautiful," the 1st deliveryman laughed as I went back into the kitchen and he started eating his food.

"Thanks Beautiful," John and 3rd deliveryman said in unison as I handed them their plates and they started eating.

"We're finished with the sectional, the entertainment center, and the dining room – now we just need to do the bedrooms," the 1st deliveryman said as he finished his food.

"Wow – you guys work fast," Jordan said.

"We're used to it," he said as they went down the hall towards the bedrooms.

"Go eat while they're finishing the bedrooms Beautiful," Jordan said.

"Okay honey," I said as I went into the kitchen. I got my plate and came back out into the living room.

"It's so beautiful," he sighed.

"Yet it is," I sighed as I finished my breakfast. We continued to stand in the living room and admire the furniture until we heard another knock on the door...

"Who is it?" Jordan asked.

"Delivery from Office Max," the man answered. Jordan looked out they keyhole and saw Carl was with him so he opened the door.

"Where to sir?" the deliveryman said.

"Wow! Who's it from?" Jordan yelled.

"Congrats on your new home and your own office! Love Marlowe," I read.

"Wow! That was so nice of Marlowe!" Jordan said.

"Your brother has good taste – this is the top of the line," the deliveryman said.

"Thank you," I said.

"This way," Jordan said as they started down the hall.

"Hey James," the deliveryman from Office Max said as the 1st deliveryman from Raymour & Flanigan passed him in the hallway.

"Hey Ron – you deliverin' furniture too?" he asked.

"Yea – I'm deliverin' the same L-Shaped Work Center you bought last week," he laughed.

"Alright – see you later man," he said as they came into the living room.

"You're all set maam," James said as they went to leave...

"Wait a minute!" I yelled.

"Something wrong maam?" James asked.

"Would you like some coffee?" I asked.

"Yes maam!" they all said in unison.

"I'll hang out here with them while you get the coffee," Jordan said as he came back down the hall.

"Okay honey," I said as I went into the kitchen to make the coffee.

"We might as well get rid of these boxes while she's makin' coffee," James said.

"Ok then," John said as they started to get the boxes together.

"All done maam," Ron said as he joined Jordan, James, John, and the 3rd deliveryman from Raymour & Flanigan in the living room.

"I'm back," I said as I handed James and John a cup of coffee. "Would you like some coffee Ron?" I asked.

"Yes maam!" he said.

"Ok then," I said as I went into the kitchen.

"So how long you been workin' for Office Max?" James asked.

"About 6 months now," Ron said.

"You like it?" James asked.

"Yea – I have better hours its closer to home, and the benefits are good," Ron said.

"Nothin' like a good job and great benefits," Jordan said as I came back into the living room with 2 cups of coffee and handed one to Ron.

"What's your name?" I asked the 3rd deliveryman from Raymour & Flanigan.

"I'm Rob, he said as he smiled at me.

"Nice meeting you Rob," I said as I handed him a cup of coffee. We were all standing there finishing our coffee when Carl was knocking on the door again...

"Who is it?" Jordan asked.

"Delivery from Macys," he answered.

"Hey Tom!" James yelled as the deliveryman came in with a flat box.

"Hey James – what brings you here?" Tom asked.

"Same thing that brings you here!" we all said in unison, then bust out laughing.

"Enjoy! Love Tim & Carolyn," Jordan read again.

"Where would you like this sir?" Tom asked.

"Right this way," Jordan said as he put the card in his pocket and Tom followed Jordan down the hall to the master bedroom.

"Y'all newlyweds?" James asked.

"Yea," I said as Jordan and Tom came back into the living room.

"Well congratulations," James said.

"Thank you," Jordan answered.

"Well we might as well get these boxes outta here," James said as he, John and Rob started to pick up the boxes.

"Might as well – I gotta lot of deliveries today," Ron said as he finished his coffee and picked up his boxes.

"Man, we been here since 8:30 this morning," James said as they all went out into the hall.

"8:30? What the hell were you delivering?" Tom asked.

"The whole damn store," James laughed as they all went towards the elevator with their boxes and got on the elevator without looking back.

"Everything's all set up for us Beautiful," Jordan said as he closed the door.

"It sure is... and we don't have to sleep on the floor anymore," I laughed.

"That gives me an idea," Jordan said seductively.

"Great minds think alike," I said as I ran down the hall and into the bedroom, threw off my robe, and jumped into the shower...

"Guess who?" Jordan said as he joined me in the shower...

"Me!" I said as I kissed him quickly, jumped out the shower, grabbed a towel, and ran towards the bedroom...

"Here I come!" Jordan said as he ran past me with a towel in his hand, tripped over my foot, and landed smack in the middle of our new bed.

"And there you go!" I laughed as I finished drying off and jumped on the bed with him.

"C'mere Beautiful," he said as he pulled me down on top of him and started kissing me...

"Let me finish drying you off," I said as I pulled the towel from underneath him and finished drying him off.

"What now Beautiful?" Jordan whispered seductively.

"Now we get some sleep... on our new bed," I yawned as I lay down on the bed beside him and we both drifted off to sleep.

Chapter 59

"Jordan! Trenice! Hello? Is Anybody Home?" Carl asked as he continued banging on the door.

"Yes Carl – we're home," Jordan laughed as he opened the door.

"I told her you weren't expecting company until 4:00 this afternoon but she insisted on coming up anyway," Carl said.

"Hi Char," I yawned as I came to the front door.

"Now see what ya made me do – ya made me wake them up – sorry for disturbing you Trenice," Carl said.

"Don't worry about it Carl – she was comin' up here regardless," I laughed.

"Well I'll add her to the visitor's list so she can come up in the future," he said. "What's your name maam?"

"I'm Charlotte – but my friends call me Char," she said as she extended her hand.

"Well I'd love to be your friend Char," Carl said as he kissed her hand.

"Oh you can definitely be my friend Carl," Char said mischievously.

"Well then, my new friend, let me give you my card so you can call me some time," Carl said.

"Thank you Carl," Char said as she put the card in her pocket.

"You have a nice day now Char," Carl said as he started backing down the hall….

"You have a nice day too Carl," Char said as she watched him backing down the hall…

"Nice meeting you Char," he said when he got to the elevator…

"Nice meeting you too Carl," she said as she watched him get in the elevator.

"What was that all about?" Jordan asked as we closed the door.

"What?" Char asked.

"You and Carl," Jordan said.

"What about me and Carl?" Char asked.

"Honey he was so cute," I laughed.

"Yes he was – he was bein' so polite n all," Jordan laughed.

"I thought it was special," Char said.

"It was Char – it was," I said.

"I wonder if he's married," Char said.

"Carl? Na, he's not married," Jordan said.

"How you know?" Char asked.

"He told me," Jordan said.

"When he tell you that?" Char asked.

"Char?" I asked, deliberately interrupting this particular conversation...

"Yea?"

"Thank you soooo much for the dinning set – it's beautiful!"

"Oh they delivered it already?"

"Yup."

"Damn – I thought I would be here before they delivered it," she laughed.

"Then you should've been here at 8:30 this morning," Jordan laughed.

"8:30? Damn!" Char laughed. "I was fryin' this fish," she said as she took it into the kitchen.

"Come check it out Char," Jordan said as she came into the dining room.

"Oh my God – it is nice!" Char said.

"And the Cupboard is perfect for china," I said.

"Or anything else you wanna put in there," Char said.

"Yea – like table cloths, napkins, place settings," Jordan said.

"So what time did they leave?" Char asked.

"About 12:00," I said.

"Damn – it took them 3 ½ hours to set this up?"

"Char you did past the living room didn't you?" Jordan asked.

"Yea..."

"Go have another look in the living room," Jordan said as we followed her...

"Oh my God! Is this the sectional your mother bought you?"

"Yup," Jordan and I said in unison.

"Oh my God! Look at this entertainment unit! This is nice!"

"Jake & Rachel bought that for us," Jordan said.

"I almost bought this for you but at the last minute I changed my mind and got the dining room set," Char laughed.

"I'm glad you did," I laughed as we followed Jordan down the hall to the office...

"Oh my God! Who bought this for you Trenice?"

"My brother."

"Nice of your brother," Char laughed.

"That's what Ron said too – and James has the same one," I laughed.

"Who's Ron and James?" she asked.

"The deliverymen from this morning," Jordan answered as we headed towards the 2nd bedroom...

"Oh my God! I almost bought this too!"

"My grandmother bought this one for us," I said.

"Wow Trenice – you did good girl," she said.

"Wait until you see this," Jordan said as he showed her into the bedroom...

"Oh my God! It's beautiful!"

"My Mum-Mum's bought this for us," Jordan beamed.

"Yea – and Carolyn & Tim bought us the flat screen tv," I said.

"Well I'ma go sit down in the living room while y'all get dressed – you want me to take the plastic off the couch?"

"No!" we both yelled in unison.

"Okay, okay," Char laughed as she went into the living room to sit down and we got dressed. Naturally, as soon as we were dressed and came down the hall we heard knockin' at the door...

"Wait a damn minute! Char said as she got up to answer the door.

"Girl, get the hell outta my way 'fore I drop this lasagna on your damn feet," Rachel laughed as she took the lasagna into the kitchen.

"Honey the entertainment center's here already," Jake said as he sat down.

"Oh my God – it's beautiful!" Rachel said.

"Thank you!" Jordan and I said in unison.

"Open the door!" Tish yelled.

"I'm comin'" Char said as she opened the door.

"Where should I put this baked ziti?" Paul asked.

"Gifts in the living room – food in the kitchen," Char said. "I might as well stay here," she laughed as we heard knockin' at the door again.

"Hey Tee, hey Joe," I said as they came in.

"Where do you want the rice & beans?" Theresa asked.

"Gifts in the living room – food in the kitchen," we all said in unison.

"Trenice this was in the fridge all night so it should be ok," Monique said as she came inside.

"What is it?" Char asked.

"Potato salad," Tim said as he went into the living room with the gift.

"Damn that fried chicken smells good," I said as Roberta came in.

"It is good," James said as he went into the living room and Roberta took the fried chicken into the kitchen.

"Damn these greens are hot," Carolyn said as she came in.

"Let me get those for you," Tim said as he took the collard greens into the kitchen.

"Hey Sherrie," I said as she headed straight to the kitchen.

"I told her to let me carry the cabbage so she wouldn't burn herself but she just had to carry it herself," Harold laughed.

"Oh shut up," Sherrie laughed as they went into the living room with their gift.

"Get your sausage & peppers!" Carlos said as he came in with Diedre.

"Carlos you go put that in the kitchen – I'll be in the living room," Diedre said as she went into the living room and sat down.

"You think this Caesar salad will be ok on the counter?" Wanda asked as she came in.

"Sure," Char said as Mike went into the living room.

"Hot corn on the cob," Scott yelled as he went straight into the kitchen.

"Hey Scott, hey Bunny," Jordan said as they went into the living room and sat down.

"I smell cornbread!" Char said as she opened the door.

"Hey everybody!" Eric said as he took the cornbread into the kitchen and Diana went into the living room.

"Oooohhhh cake!" I yelled as Grandma came in with a cake and a bag of gifts.

"Hi Grandma!" everybody said in unison.

"Is there room for this in the kitchen?" she asked.

"You can put that on the island Grandma," I said.

"Jordan come take one of these tins of macaroni & cheese," my mother said as she came in.

"Hi Miss Claire!" everyone yelled in unison.

"Hi Jordan! Hi Trenice!" Shaliyah yelled as she came in behind my mother.

"Hi Shaliyah!" everyone yelled in unison.

"Hey everybody!" Marlowe said as he came in.

"Hey Marlowe!" we all yelled in unison.

"Hey Trenice," Miss Birdie said as she came in. I heard you was havin' a party.

"Well hello Miss Birdie," Jordan said.

"I brought you some koolaid – you know you gotsa have koolaid…"

"Cause everybody don't drink!" we all yelled in unison, then bust out laughing.

"Well here's the pitcher, and here's some ice," Miss April said as they came in.

"Hi Mum-Mum!" we all said in unison.

"Jordan, help us put this liquor in the kitchen 'fore we drop these bottles," Miss June laughed.

"Well we might as well get started," Char said.

"Welcome to our housewarming everyone," Jordan said. "Before we begin the festivities I'd like to thank everyone for their gifts. The sectional you are all sitting on is our gift from Ma," Jordan said.

"The dining room set is our gift from Char," I said.

"The entertainment center is our gift from Jake & Rachel," Jordan said.

"If you'll follow us down the hall to the master bedroom, we'll continue with the presentation," I said.

"This bedroom set, complete with a king mattress and box spring, is our gift from Mum-Mum and this flat screen tv is our gift from Tim & Carolyn," Jordan said.

"This bedroom set, complete with a king mattress and box spring, is our gift from Grandma and this office furniture is our gift from Marlowe," I said.

"And now we'll continue with the presentation in the living room," Jordan said as everyone followed us back down the hall.

"Who is it?" I said as I went to the door.

"You have another delivery Trenice," Carl said.

"Thank you Carl," I said as I took the bag from him.

"You're welcome. I'll be downstairs if you need me," he said as he closed the door.

"We can start with these," I said as I pulled out the gift and tore off the wrapping paper. "Style & Co. 300 Thread Count Egyptian Cotton Sheet Set – one in honey and one in ivory," I read.

"Who's it from?" Jordan asked.

"Le'me read the card... Enjoy! Love Vanessa."

"Who's Vanessa?" Tish asked.

"She's our real estate agent," I said.

"I wonder what this is," I asked as I pulled out an envelope... "Oh look – it's a bill from Tyler," I laughed as I ripped it open and read... "This one's on me – balance = 0 Love Tyler."

"Oh that was nice! Miss April said.

"I wonder that these are," Jordan said as he took the remaining gifts out the bag and tore off the paper… "Uniden 5.8GHZ Digital Phone/Answering System – one corded, one cordless," Jordan read.

"Oh that's perfect – we didn't even think to buy phones," I laughed.

"And now you won't have to," Miss June laughed.

"Ok my turn," Grandma said.

"Ok Grandma!" we all yelled in unison as she gave me the bag and I took 2 gifts out the bag.

"Thank you Miss Gladys," Jordan said.

"Those aren't from me," she said.

"Who are they from Grandma?" I asked.

"Open them and find out," she said.

"Style & Co. Reversible Solid Towel Set – one in jade and one in ocean… Enjoy! Love Sissy," I read.

"Wow that was nice of her," Char said.

"It certainly was," Jordan said.

"Warmsutta Palace Classic 12 Piece Bath Set… Enjoy! Love Aunt Trudy," I read.

"Trudy? Wow – that's a surprise," Jordan said.

"Yes it is," I said.

"I wanna go next!" my sister Shaliyah said.

"Ok Shaliyah!" we all said in unison.

"Oh Shaliyah – these are beautiful – thank you!" I said as we hugged each other.

"Aww…" everyone said as Jordan held up the key chains that had 'Welcome Home' on them.

"Let's put these on our key's now honey," I said.

"Ok," Jordan said as he put our keys on our new key chains.

"I knew you wouldn't be able to guess," Shaliyah laughed.

"You were right Shaliyah – and no one else bought us keychains," I said.

"Me next," Miss Birdie said as she handed Jordan her gift and he tore off the paper...

"CHF Sahara Blue Window Collection Curtains," Jordan read. "These are very nice – thank you Miss Birdie," he said.

"You're welcome," she said.

"They're the perfect match to the sectional," I said.

"Next," Diana said as she handed me her gift and I tore off the paper...

"Sharper Image Blue Night CD Stero," I read.

"Very nice! Thank you!" Jordan said.

"We knew you didn't have one," Eric said.

"Next!" Scott said as he gave Jordan and I a gift and we tore off the paper...

"Cuisinart Brushed Stainless Steel Smart Power Premier Blender," Jordan read.

"Now that's the perfect blender for the bartender," my mother laughed.

"Cuisinart Classic Brushed Chrome 4 Slice Toaster," I read.

"Aww shit – you ain't had toast until you've had a classic slice," Joe laughed.

"Next!" Mike said as he gave Jordan and I a gift and we tore off the paper...

"Sunbeam Iron," I read.

"Conair Compact Presser with Removable Water Tank & Pressing Pad," Jordan read.

"Oh this is perfect – I won't have to put my suits in the cleaners," Jordan said.

"A man's gotta look good when he goes in the streets," Mike said.

"What the fuck you tryin' a say Mike?" Wanda snapped.

"Why you gotta start shit every time we go somewhere?" Mike snapped.

"You the one startin' shit talkin' 'bout a man's gotta look good when he goes in the streets... like you don't look good when you go out," she snapped.

"I know I look good when I go out – and Jordan will too," he said.

"I'm the one that knows you look good when you go out in the streets 'cause I'm the one that presses your damn suits – don't be tryin' a say you know you look good when you know damn well if it wasn't for me..."

"Yes baby – you make sure your man looks damn good when he goes outside," he said as he pulled her into a kiss.

"That's better," she said as she kissed him back.

"Next!" Carlos said as he gave Jordan and I a gift and we tore off the paper...

"LaCrosse Wireless Atomic Clock with Weather and Forecast," I read.

"HoMedics Sound Spa Classic Deluxe Clock Radio and Sound Machine," Jordan read.

"Oh that's nice – it lulls you to sleep," Rachel said.

"Perfect – this one for the bedroom and the other one for the kitchen," I said.

"Next!" Harold said as he placed a big box in our lap and we tore off the paper...

"Sharp Warm & Toasty Microwave Toaster Oven Combo," Jordan read.

"Oh wow! That's really nice! Thank you!" I said.

"Next!" Roberta said as James placed a large box in our lap and we tore off the paper...

"20 Piece KitchenAid Distinctions Cookware Set," I read.

"A man's gotta eat," James said.

"And this man will eat," Jordan laughed.

"Next!" Monique said as Khoury placed a large box in our lap and we tore off the paper...

"Oh my God! It's Beautiful!" I yelled.

"Royal Doulton Countess 20 Piece Dinnerware," Jordan read.

"This can go right in the Cupboard in the dining room," I said.

"It's really beautiful – thank you," Jordan said.

"Everyone should have a set of china," Monique said.

"Say that shit after you have kids," my mother said as we all bust out laughing.

"Next!" Theresa said as Joe placed a large box in our lap and we tore off the paper...

"Oh these are beautiful!" Jordan said.

"Lenox Pearl Platinum 20 Piece Stemware," I read.

"They'll look so nice in the Cupboard with the china," Theresa said.

"Yes they will – thank you," I said.

"Here ya go!" Tish yelled as Paul placed a gift in my lap and I tore off the paper...

"Oh my God Tish... how did you know?" I asked with tears in my eyes...

"Lenox TinCanAlley 65 Piece Sterling Silver Flatware Set with Caddy Service for 12," Jordan read.

"Aww... that's nice!" Miss April said.

"I knew Char bought you the dining room with the Cupboard and I knew you were getting china and stemware," Tish said.

"Thank you everybody," I said with tears in my eyes.

"Aww... your welcome," everyone said in unison as Jordan kissed me.

"Aiight – we got koolaid on ice, liquor, and plenty of food – let's eat," Miss Birdie said as she got up and went in the kitchen.

"Let's eat!" we all said in unison as we followed her into the kitchen and helped ourselves.

"Claire, you playin' spades?" Miss April yelled.

"I sure am," my mother yelled as she went into the dining room.

"Where's your partner?" Miss June asked.

"Right here," I said as I sat down.

"Alrighty then! Let's get this party started!" Miss April said as we started playing. It was only 5 hands and it was no contest.

"I swear – I hate playin' against these two!" Miss June said.

"Next!" my mother said as Miss Birdie sat down.

"Where's your partner?" I laughed.

"Right here," Grandma said as she sat down.

"Aww shit!" everyone said in unison. It was no contest for them either.

"Sorry Ma," my mother said.

"Shut the hell up Claire," my grandmother laughed.

"You still got game Grandma," I laughed.

"You only beat us by 5 damn points," she laughed.

"A win is a win," my mother laughed.

"Try that shit now," Tish said as she sat down.

"Bring it!" my mother said as Paul sat down. This time they had the cards...

"Ahem! The new undefeated spades champions are..."

"Us!" Joe said as he sat down. "Let's show 'em how it's done Tee," Joe said.

"Let's do this!" Theresa said as she sat down.... And took Tish's crown...

"What were you saying about being undefeated?" Joe laughed.

"They were sayin' we gonna bust dat ass!" Khoury said as he and Monique sat down... and that's exactly what they did...

"Who's next?" Khoury asked.

"You," James said as he and Robert sat down.

"We'll see about that," Khoury said as they played their hands...

"Like I said – you were next," James laughed as they beat them in the last hand.

"Enjoy it while it lasts," Carolyn said as she and Tim sat down and began to play. It didn't last long for them at all...

"Aiight – who has what it takes to take the title?" Carolyn asked.

"We do," Sherrie said as she and Harold sat down to play... and that's exactly what they did...

"You wanna piece of me Diedre?" Sherrie asked as she and Carlos sat down to play...

"Oh I'm gonna get a piece of you alright," she said as they continued to play... and get a piece she did...

"It's on now," Mike said as he and Wanda sat down...

"It won't be for long," Carlos said.

"You're right – 'cause you'll be gettin' up from this table in about 2 more hands," Mike laughed... and that's exactly what happened...

"Bet your ass can't do that shit again," Scott said as he and Bunny sat down to play..."

"Bet your ass I will do that again," Mike laughed as they won the first hand.

"Try it again," Bunny said as they won the 2nd hand.

"I just did," Wanda said as they won the 3rd hand.

"And the reigning champions are... Mike & Wanda," Mike said as they won the 4th hand and ended the game.

"So far we have a tie – Mike & Wanda with 2 wins – Miss Claire & Trenice with 2 wins. Diana & Eric are up next," Char said as Diana & Eric sat down to play.

"In your dreams," Diana said as she and Eric played against Mike and Wanda. It was pitiful.

"3 hands – you losin' your touch Mike?" Eric asked.

"It ain't over yet," Mike said as they got up from the table.

"It will be soon though," Diana said as Jake and Rachel sat down to play. Unfortunately, she was right – it was over soon – for them.

"Hate to do it to ya Diana but that's how it be sometimes," Rachel said.

"That's aiight – we'll get a rematch," Eric said.

"Not tonight," Jake laughed.

"Alrighty – we have a tie – Mike & Wanda with 2 wins – Miss Claire & Trenice with 2 wins. Whoever wins this next round will be the champions!" Char yelled as we sat down at the table to play against Wanda and Mike.

"That's aiight – Miss Claire n Trenice gonna bust yo' ass!" Diana yelled.

"They can try," Wanda said as we sat down to play with them. It didn't take long...

"And we retain our crowns," my mother said as we high-fived.

"Go 'head with your bad self Claire," Miss Birdie said.

"Congrats Beautiful," Jordan said as he pulled me into a kiss.

"Thank you Honey," I said as I kissed him back.

"Claire n Trenice are tough to beat," Miss April said.

"That's aiight – we'll have our day," Wanda said.

"Not tonight!" my mother and I laughed.

"Try that shit again next week," Rachel said.

"Ok," I yawned.

"Well we might as well get goin'," Miss Birdie said. "Besides – I gotta git to the store and git my number in 'fore it come out so I can get paid," she laughed.

"You might as well quit," Miss June laughed.

"Shiiiitttt – ain't nobody ever tell you you can't win if you don't play?" Miss Birdie laughed.

"You been playin' for years – you ain't won nothin' and you ain't gonna win nothin'" Miss June laughed.

"I wouldn't go that far June – she'll remember that shit when she **DOES** win and she won't give you shit," my grandmother laughed.

"Let her keep talkin' Gladys," Miss Birdie laughed. "I'ma go put these numbers in 'fore the store close – congrats you two," she said as she hugged Jordan and me.

"Thank you Miss Birdie," Jordan said.

"Well we might as well get going too," my grandmother said as she hugged us. "Don't forget my number Trenice," she said.

"I won't Grandma," I said.

"We're gonna go too," Miss April said as she and Miss June hugged us.

"Bye Mum-Mum," Jordan said as we all hugged.

"Bye Miss April... bye Miss June...," I yawned.

"Well we might as well get goin'... Trenice can't hang no more," my mother laughed.

"Good night everybody," Jordan said as everyone left but Jake, Rachel, and Char.

"You did good today," Jake said.

"We sure did," Jordan yawned.

"Oh boy – let's put this food away and clean up so they can go to bed," Char laughed.

"Ok Char," Rachel said as they all headed in the kitchen and Jordan I headed down the hall to the bedroom, collapsed on the bed, and fell asleep watching our new flat screen tv while they were cleaning up and putting the food away.

"Honey look at these two," Rachel whispered to Jake as they watched us sleeping.

"Reminds me of when you and I first moved in together," Jake whispered.

"Why y'all whispering?" Char said as she came down the hall....

"Ssshhhh!" they said in unison as Char tiptoed to the door and peeked into the bedroom.

"Aww... they look so cute," Char whispered.

"They had a long, long, day," Jake said as they all went down the hall.

"They been up since 8:30 this morning, Char said as they went out the door and closed it behind them.

"What the hell were they doing up so early?" Rachel asked.

"Deliveries," Char said.

"Damn – Raymour & Flanigan deliver before 9 a.m.?" Rachel asked.

"Probably not – but since they were bringin' the whole store they probably figured they'd need the whole morning to deliver and set everything up," Char laughed.

"I bet they did too," Jake laughed as they got onto the elevator.

"They did – they didn't leave until almost 12," Char said.

"Damn!" Rachel said as they got off the elevator.

"Have a good afternoon Char," Carl said as they went into the lobby.

"Thank you – you too Carl," Char said as they left.

Chapter 60

Jordan and I spent Saturday night and all day Sunday eating, sleeping, and putting everything away. We didn't realize how tired we were until Monday morning...

"Wake up honey," I yawned as I looked at the clock to see what time it was.

"What time is it?" Jordan yawned.

"Looks like 7:30," I yawned.

"I guess I gotta get up then," Jordan said as he got up and went into the bathroom. When he stepped into the Jacuzzi and turned on the shower I just stood there watching him for a few minutes...

"I wish you could join me Beautiful."

"I wish I could too – but it won't be long now," I yawned. "Besides – I don't wanna push it – bad enough I got this cast wet as it is."

"It'll be alright – besides you weren't in here that long."

"After I see Dr. Campton I can be in there as long as I want to," I yawned.

"Sounds good," he said.

"I have a lot to do today and I can't wait to get this cast off...

"I'ma go now – call me later Beautiful," he said as he went down the hall and out the door.

"I will... I love you honey."

"I love you too – see you tonight Beautiful."

I finished getting dressed and went downstairs.

"Mornin' Trenice," Carl said as I went into the lobby.

"Mornin' Carl – have a nice day," I said as I left.

The bus pulled up just as my leg started bothering me. "Thank God," I said as it pulled up and I got on. I went straight to the back, found a comfortable seat, and stretched my leg out all the way to White Plains. Fortunately Dr. Campton's office wasn't too far from where I got off and it was a nice day so I stopped at Starbucks to get a Grande Carmel Machiatta before I got to his office.

"Good morning," I said to the receptionist.

"Good morning Trenice," she said as she pulled my chart.

"Busy today?" I said as I sat down.

"Busy every Monday," she said without looking up from the chart.

"Interesting reading?" I asked.

"Not really – I just noticed that you're scheduled to get your cast off today," she said.

"Yes I am and I can't wait!" I said.

"You may have to," she said.

"Dr. Campton not here yet?" I asked.

"He's at the hospital – he had an emergency surgery – he may not be in until this afternoon – actually I was supposed to cancel your appointment and reschedule you for tomorrow," she said.

"Are you fuckin' kiddn' me?" I asked.

"I know – I'm sorry Trenice – I'll let him know you're here when he calls in," she said.

"Oh well," I sighed as I turned on Jerry Springer. "At least I won't be bored," I said as I watched Jerry Springer. Dr. Campton finally called after I finished watching Maury...

"Hi Dr. Campton... uhuh... Trenice is here... uhuh... ok I'll let her know..."

"He's not coming back?" I asked.

"He'll be here in a few minutes," she said.

I got about ½ way through the 2nd Jerry Springer when he came in...

"Hello Trenice! Good to see you!" he said.

"Good to see you too!" I laughed.

"Cut the shit – you just wanna get that damn cast off," he laughed. "Come on in," he said as he stopped to pick up my chart. I followed him into the office and sat down in the chair.

"Trenice I need you to get up on the table," he said.

"I'd like too – but I overdid it a bit this weekend," I laughed as he helped me up onto the table.

"Danced your ass off eh?" he laughed as he started removing the cast..."

"Naaa... Jordan and I moved into our home this weekend," I said.

"Well now I know how your cast got wet," he laughed. "So are you all settled in?" he asked.

"Yea... ouch!" I said as he bent my leg and rotated my foot.

"Have you eaten yet?" he asked.

"No – just coffee," I said.

"Here," he said as he handed me 2 motrin. "I wanna take an x-ray just to make sure everything's ok then you can go," he said as he went to get the x-ray machine. When he came back into the room he took a couple of x-rays and I sat there waiting while he read the x-rays, wrote something in my chart, then looked at the x-rays again.

"Something wrong?" I asked.

"I'm not sure – it's probably nothing but I want you to go over to the hospital for an MRI just to be on the safe side," he said.

"Why?"

"As I said – it's probably nothing – but I want to make sure – here's your shoes", he said as he put them on my feet and helped me down off the table.

"Thanks Dr. Campton," I said as I went back out into the reception area.

"Your welcome Trenice – and congrats on your new home," he said.

"New home?" the receptionist asked.

"Yea..." I sighed.

"Congratulations," she said.

"Thank you," I said.

"Carol – call the MRI unit at the hospital and tell them I'm sending Trenice over for an MRI of her leg – and give Trenice a prescription so they don't give her a hard time," he said as he went back into his office.

"Here ya go Trenice," she said as she handed me the prescription. "Congrats again."

"Thanks," I said as I left Dr. Campton's office and headed for White Plains Hospital. When I got there I didn't have to wait long.

"Hi Trenice – come on in," the receptionist said as I walked into the lobby.

"You remembered me – how nice," I said.

"Just remove everything from the bottom down and go on in," she said.

"Hello Trenice," the technician said as I got up on the table. "Do you know why the Dr. asked for an MRI?"

"No," I said as I laid down, waiting to be moved into the tube....

"It's probably nothing but he just wants an MRI to be on the safe side," he said as he put me in the tube.

"Yea – that's what he said," I said as he left the room and started taking the pictures.

"Oh so you do know why you're here then," he said.

"Not really – but as long as the MRI is good I'm good," I said as he removed me from the tube and helped me down from the table.

"I'll get these to Dr. Campton before the week is out and he'll get a report from me later today – he'll call you if anything's wrong," he said as I left the room.

"Ok thanks," I said as I finished getting dressed and left the hospital. "Shit – it's almost 1:00 – I better get something to eat before I fall down," I said as I headed for the Galleria and went down to the food court. After I finished eating I did some window shopping in JC Penney, Macy's Victoria's Secret, and Kay Jewlers. My leg started bothering me again so I figured I'd treat myself to a manicure, pedicure, and massage. By the time I was done, it was a little after 5... "Oh my God – it's after 5 – le'me call Jordan and let him know I'm on my way," I said as I went downstairs to get the bus.

"Hello?"

"Hi Honey."

"Hey Beautiful. You on your way home yet?"

"I just left the Galleria," I said as I got on the #60 bus. "I'm gonna stop at the Food Emporium and pick up dinner and dessert."

"Hurry home Beautiful – I miss you so bad it hurts."

"I miss you. I can't wait for us to finally be together in our bed in our home," I sighed.

"I hear ya girl," I heard from the seat behind me.

"Neither can I... hold on a minute... hello? Yea Jake – le'me call you back after I get off the phone with Trenice... uhuh...ok," he laughed as he got back on the phone with me.

"What was that all about?" I asked.

"That was Jake – he said call him if we need him."

"Why would we need him?"

"In case we break our new bed," he laughed.

"Oh he's so funny," I laughed. "When I was telling you I couldn't wait for us to finally be together in our bed in our home the girl in back of me said, "I hear ya girl!" like I was talkin' to her!" I laughed.

"I guess you were talkin' to her too – maybe you should've invited her over," Jordan laughed.

"Hell no – she probably would've accepted the invitation," I laughed. I could see her cuttin' her eyes at me from the seat across from me but I didn't give a shit. Far as I was concerned she should've stayed out my conversation. "Well I'm gettin' off now – I'll call you back when I'm on my way home," I said as I got off the bus.

"I'll see you soon Beautiful."

"I love you."

"I love you too."

"I'm so excited I don't know what I wanna do first," I said as I hurried around the Food Emporium. All I could think about was Jordan and I in our new home.

"Excuse me!" she blurted out interrupting my thoughts.

"You're excused," I said matter-of-factly and went back to looking on the shelf.

"Well are you gonna get the hell outta my way or what?" she snapped.

"I can't do a damn thing about hell being in your way," I laughed as I continued looking on the shelf. "Hmm… why is it that they never have Barilla spaghetti when I want it?" I asked out loud while I continued to ignore her, trying hard not to laugh…

"Oh you think you fuckin' funny don't you?" she snapped.

"Oh I know I'm funny," I laughed. "And I'll be fuckin' later tonight – you wanna stop by?"

"Clean up in isle 3!" the stockman yelled as he bent over laughing, holding his stomach, and backing away from the jar of spaghetti sauce he dropped on the floor.

"I don't have time for this – **WOULD YOU PLEASE MOVE YOUR CART**?" she snapped as the stockman and I continued laughing.

"My cart isn't in your way – you can go around me," I said matter-of-factly as I took a box of Barilla spaghetti off the shelf along with a jar of spaghetti sauce, put it in my cart, and proceeded down the aisle.

"Fuck this!" she yelled as she shoved past me, banged into my cart, slipped on the spaghetti sauce, and hit the floor. That did it.

"Are you ok maam?" the stockman asked, trying not to laugh.

"You okaaayyy?" I teased as I walked past her with my cart without looking back. "That's what the fuck you get for being such a bitch," I said as I turned and went into the next isle. "Now let's see – where was I before I was so rudely interrupted – oh yes – dinner and dessert," I said as I picked up some vanilla ice cream, cherries, chocolate syrup, nuts, sprinkles, and whipped cream. "Can't forget the garlic bread," I said as I picked up a loaf of garlic bread with cheese and placed it in the cart. "All I need is the salad and I'm done," I said as I continued down the aisle. "Caesar... perfect!" I said as I picked up the bag and placed it in the cart. "Ok – now let's get some ground beef," I said as I went to pick up a package of ground beef and the bitch grabbed it first.

"Ha ha bitch!" she yelled as she grabbed the ground beef.

I took one look at her white pants and the spaghetti sauce all over them from when she fell in the isle and bust out laughing. "Nice pants!" I yelled as I grabbed another package of ground beef, placed it in the cart, and continued walking down the aisle. "I can't wait to get outta here," I said as I grabbed a bag of chopped onions and peppers and placed them in the cart. "Hope the lines aren't too bad," I said as I picked up two bottles of Pepsi and placed them in the cart. I started walking towards the checkout and saw the grated parmesan cheese. "Good thing I saw this – I almost forgot it," I said as I picked up a can, placed it in the cart, and proceeded to check out. "Let's see – I can go in the express line – good," I said as I got in line behind the bitch.

"Oh boy.... I sure hope I have everything... you know sometimes you forget something and you have to go back and get it – then you hold up the line 'cause you can't find it – or sometimes you don't have a price on your item and they have to call someone to go do a price check... I sure hope that doesn't happen today 'cause I don't wanna **PISS ANYONE OFF!**" she yelled as she got in my face.

"**Aaaaahhhhhhchoooo!**" I said as I pretended to sneeze, spitting in her face as I did so.

"Do you need a tissue maam?" the lady said as she came up from behind me and handed me a tissue.

"Thank you," I said as I took the tissue from her and wiped my mouth and nose while hiding my smirk from the bitch.

"Fuckin' bitch – that's your ass when we get outside," she said as she put her things on the conveyor belt.

"Security!" the lady yelled from behind me.

"We got a problem here?" he asked as he came upon us.

"Yes – that lady just threatened her," she said as she pointed to the bitch and then to me.

"I ain't do shit yet," she said as she put her bagged groceries in her cart.

"Did she threaten you maam?" he asked me.

"No she didn't threaten me – she's pissed because the stockman dropped a jar of spaghetti sauce in isle 3 and she slipped and fell in it," I laughed as I pointed at her pants.

"Damn – she got on white pants – I'd be pissed too," he laughed. "Well - have a nice evening ladies," he said as he walked towards the exit.

"Thank you, same to you," I said as I put my bagged groceries in the cart and followed him to the exit.

"Would you like me to call a cab for you?"

"Yes – Thank You!"

"My pleasure maam – where too?"

"I'm going to 34 South Broadway," the lady said as she came up behind me.

"I'm going to Yonkers," I laughed.

"I need two cabs at the Food Emporium on Mamaroneck Avenue – one local, one out of town," he said as the bitch looked on. "You need a cab maam?" he asked her.

"Yea," she said rudely.

"Here's your cab maam," he said as he opened the door for the lady behind me but the bitch jumped in the cab before she could reach the door and slammed it shut. "Guess she needs to hurry home and change those pants," he said as we all bust out laughing.

"No matter – I wasn't in a hurry anyway," the lady said as she got in the next cab that pulled up.

"Here's your cab maam," he said as he held the door open for me.

"Thanks," I said as I got in the cab.

"You have a good night," he said as the driver finished putting the bags in the trunk and got back in the cab.

"Thanks again," I said as we pulled away from the Food Emporium.

"Where to?" the driver asked.

"Yonkers," I said as we rode down Mamaroneck Avenue.

"Ok," he said as we pulled into the Getty Station.

"Why are we stopping here?" I asked.

"Gotta get some gas and check the engine," he said as he got out the cab. "I'll just be a few minutes," he said as he started to check under the hood.

"Oh well, beats walkin'," I said as I leaned back in the seat and he closed the hood. "Le'me call Jordan and let him know I'm on my way," I said as I dialed my number.

"Hello"

"Hi Honey."

"Hey Beautiful. You on your way?"

"Yea – I'm in the cab now – he just stopped at the station to get some gas and check the engine."

"Won't be long now," he said.

"He's on his way back now – I'll be home in a little while – I love you."

"I love you to Beautiful," he said as he hung up.

"Now where the hell is he going?" I asked as the driver went inside the station. "He better not take all night either," I said as I slumped back in the seat and waited a few more minutes. "Shit – it's almost 6:30 – what the hell is he doing in there?" I asked as I looked at my watch. "Oh well – long as he's in there I'ma go to the bathroom," I said as I got out the cab and went inside. "Hello? Anybody in here?" I yelled as I pushed the door open to the bathroom. "I guess not," I said as I lifted up my skirt pulled down my panties, and squatted over the toilet. "Damn I had to go," I said as I peed in the toilet. "Why these bathrooms gotta be so nasty anyway – oh well – good thing I didn't have to take a shit – I'da been in trouble," I laughed as I grabbed the last bit of toilet paper, wiped myself, and flushed the toilet. "Shit – must be gettin' dark – I can barely see," I said as I started to pull up my panties.

"Don't move," he said as I looked up.
I couldn't move if I wanted to. My legs were paralyzed as I stood over the toilet with my panties down at my ankles. I couldn't take a breath. I couldn't make out his face. I could, however, see the reflection of the moon very clearly in the knife he had in his hand as the light of the moon came in through the window. I followed the reflection of the moon in the knife from left to right with my eyes... Left... Right... Left... Right... Left... Right... Left... Right... Run....

"Try that shit again and I'll fuckin' kill you," he whispered as he shoved me back against the wall over the toilet, knocking my pocketbook off my shoulder and onto the floor while holding the knife against my throat. When he was finished he backed away from me and zipped up his pants. I followed the reflection of the moon in the knife from left to right again with my eyes... Left... Right... Left... Right... Left...

Right… Left… Right… Turn… Down… I kicked off my panties and kept my eyes on the reflection of the moon in the knife on the sink as he continued to fix his clothes with his back to me. Just as he started to turn towards me again I grabbed the cover off the back of the toilet and commenced to swinging…

"Bang!" the sound echoed off the walls as I hit him upside his head…

"You're dead bitch!" he said as I swung again…

"Bang!" the sound echoed off the walls as I hit him upside his head again…

"Thud!" the sound echoed as he lunged for me again, missing me as I backed away, hitting the floor, too stunned to get up and try again…

"DON'T! YOU! EVER! FUCKIN'! TOUCH! ME! AGAIN! DON'T! YOU! EVER! FUCKIN'! TOUCH! ME! AGAIN! DON'T! YOU! EVER! FUCKIN'! TOUCH! ME! AGAIN!" I yelled as I continued to bash his head in until the cover broke into pieces.

I stood there looking down at his body, daring him to move, daring him to breathe. When he didn't do either I kicked him in the head then jumped back away from him, expecting him to get up.

"Oh shit… I think he's dead," I laughed as I slumped down against the wall. "What time is it anyway?" I said as I tried to look at my watch. "Shit – I can't see a fuckin' thing in here – le'me get the fuck outta here," I said as I got up and went outside. "Shit – it's 7:30 – Jordan's gotta be worried – I gotta get home," I said as I went towards the cab and tried to open the trunk. "Shit, Shit, Shit, Shit, Shit! Now what the fuck am I gonna do?" I said as I started to cry. "C'mon Trenice," I said as I started to fan myself... "Get a hold of yourself... think.... think.... think.... I got it!" I yelled as I ran back into the bathroom and turned on the light.

"Oh my God," I whispered. I had no idea what I'd done before I ran out the bathroom but now that the door was open and the light was on there was no denying it. The cab driver lay in a pool of blood in the middle of the floor. His head was a bloody mess. There were bits and pieces of bloody ceramic everywhere. The knife was on the sink right where he left it. I tiptoed over to his body and knelt down. I reached in his left pocket and pulled out his wallet. There wasn't any ID in it but there was a wad of cash. "I'll take this," I said as I took the cash out and threw the empty wallet across the bathroom. I reached in his right pocket and pulled out his keys. "Now I can get the fuck outta here," I said as I got up, went over to the toilet, picked up my pocketbook, put it on my shoulder, went towards the door, turned out the light, and ran outside to the cab.

"C'mon, c'mon, c'mon, c'mon, c'mon!" I yelled as I kept trying keys in the lock until I finally got the trunk open. I snatched my groceries out of the trunk, threw the keys over the fence, and began running towards the bus stop. "Thank God," I said as the #60 pulled up.

"Evening maam," the driver said as I stepped inside the bus and sat down.

"I'll pay the fare soon as I catch my breath," I said as I clutched my chest.

"Last stop is the station - you only have three stops - don't worry about it," he said as he turned onto Martine Avenue.

"Thanks," I said as I began to calm down, until he saw the blood.

"What's that you got on your foot? Looks like blood – you need a doctor maam?" He said as he pulled into the Trans center. "No, no – I'm ok – an animal got hit by a car on Mamaroneck Avenue and when I was running for the bus I didn't see it," I lied.

"Must'a been a big animal – was it a dog?" he asked as he stopped and opened the door.

"Yea that's it – a dog," I lied. "Thanks again," I said as I hurried off the bus and ran across the street to the Metro North train station with my groceries.

"I gotta get rid of these fuckin' shoes," I said out loud as I took them off and threw them in the first trash can I saw. That's when I saw the black cab.

"You need a taxi maam?"

I didn't answer. I just screamed and ran towards the entrance to the train station.

"You need help?" the officer asked as I got to the door.

"I gotta train to catch," I lied as I ran into the station and started up the escalator with my groceries.

"Here – let me help you," the officer said as he caught up to me and took my bags out of my hand.

"Thanks."

"You sure you're ok?"

"Yea."

"I couldn't help but notice – you ran away from that cab screaming..."

"Yea – I wasn't watching where I was running and he almost hit me," I lied.

"Oh I see," he laughed. "Didn't bother going back for your shoes huh?"

"Naa... you know how it is when people walk their dog – just my luck I had to step in it – completely ruined my shoes," I lied.

"Where'd this happen? They still down there?" he asked.

"It happened right down stairs where I came in," I lied, praying he'd go downstairs, look for the dog, and leave me alone.

"Your train will be here in a few minutes – I'll be right back," he said as he started down the escalator.

"The train to 125th Street – Grand Central Terminal – is arriving on track 2," the loud speaker echoed as everyone went up towards the platform.

"Thank you Lord," I said as I boarded the train.

"Last call for 125th Street – Grand Central Terminal," the loud speaker echoed as the doors closed and we left the station. I could see the police officer walking up and down the platform as we left.

"Tickets please," the conductor said as he came towards me.

"Shit – I forgot to buy a damn ticket!" I said as he stopped in front of me.

"That's ok maam - you can just pay me in cash – you know there's a penalty because you didn't buy your ticked before you boarded the train," he said as he took my $20 bill and handed me the change.

"Yes I know."

"So where you headed?"

"Yonkers."

"You can't get to Yonkers from here. You need to go to 125th Street and switch over to the Hudson Line."

"I know."

"Ok then – we should be there in a few minutes."

"Thank you."

When we got to 125th Street I didn't have to wait long – just as I was leaving one train the other one was boarding. "Last call for Yonkers, Glenwood…"

"Waaaiiiittt!" I yelled as I grabbed my groceries and ran towards the door.

"Another second maam and you would've missed it," the conductor laughed as I sat down to catch my breath. "I don't suppose you have a ticket?"

"You suppose right," I said as I handed him a $20 bill.

"I suppose you know there's a penalty for not buying your ticket before boarding?"

"You suppose right again."

"So where you headed?"

"Yonkers."

"Ok – have a good evening," he said as he gave me my change and walked away.

I continued to look out the window until I heard, "Yonkers next," then I stood up, picked up my groceries, and went towards the door.

"Night maam," the conductor said as I left the train with the other passengers. I was ok until I got downstairs and saw the cabs.

"Taxi?" the doorman asked me.

"No thanks," I said as I pushed passed him.

"I need a taxi – I'm going to 655 North Broadway," the lady yelled behind me…"

"Right this way maam," the doorman said as he opened the door for her.

"Mind if I share your cab? I'm going the same way," I said as I got in and sat next to her."

"Can't you get your own cab?" she snapped.

"I hate to ride alone," I lied. "Besides – the driver can get two fares," I said as I closed the door.

"Whatever!" she snapped as he started to pull off. "Just make sure you drop me off first 'cause technically it is my cab," she said.

"Where too maam?" the driver asked.

"600 North Broadway," I said.

"Hey! This is my cab – I should get dropped off first!" she yelled.

"Why would I drive past 600 to drop you off at 655?" the driver asked.

"I'll pay for both of us," I said as I handed him a $10 bill.

"You didn't say you were treating," she said as the driver pulled up in front of our building. I got out the cab, slammed the door, and went inside without looking back.

Chapter 61

"Evening Trenice," Carl said as I hurried into the building.

"Hi Carl," I said as I headed for the elevator.

"Let me get those for you," He said as he tried to take the bags from me.

"No!" I shouted as I snatched the bags. "I'm sorry Carl – I haven't had a very good day – I didn't mean to snap like that," I said. That was the first thing I'd said all evening that was actually the truth.

"I kinda figured the way you were hurrying into the building 'n all – go upstairs and tell Jordan I said to draw you a warm bath and massage your feet while he's at it – where the hell are your shoes anyway?" he asked as I got into the elevator.

"Gone," I said as the door closed in his face and I headed up to the 14th floor. I slumped down onto the floor with my face in my hands. "How am I ever gonna get through this?" I whispered, oblivious to the doors opening.

"Trenice what happened?" Jordan asked as he came into the elevator with the elderly couple down the hall from us.

"I'm ok – I just need to get inside and get outta these clothes," I lied as he helped me up and grabbed the groceries.

"I missed you Beautiful," he said as he pulled me into a kiss and I started to cry. "What's wrong Trenice?"

"I missed you too," I said as we started down the hall towards our door.

"Stop it!" I yelled as I turned to face him.

"Trenice what's wrong with you?" he asked with tears in his eyes...

"Honey I'm sorry," I said as I pulled him into a kiss. "I didn't have a good day, you know how it is when you go shopping, I had to throw my shoes in the garbage, the ice cream melted all over the soda, I need to get the onions, peppers, salad, and cherries in the fridge..." I couldn't hold it in any longer...

"Oh my God Trenice – it's just food," Jordan said as he held me and I cried on his shoulder.

"I just wanted everything to be perfect," I cried as he stroked my hair.

"Everything is perfect," he said as he picked up my face and kissed me. "We're here. Together. I don't give a damn about the food," he said as he pulled my face to his and kissed me passionately. "I just want to be with you."

"I wanna be with you too," I whispered as I started crying again.

"Now that's more like it," he said as he started to lift up my skirt. "Trenice what the hell is this on your skirt? Is this blood?"

"No," I lied. "When I was in the Food Emporium the stockman dropped a jar of spaghetti sauce in isle 3 and it splattered all over me," I lied as I took off my skirt and threw it in the garbage. "You should've been there – another lady got impatient and tried to shove her cart past me and she slipped and fell right in it – she had on white pants too," I said as I took off my blouse and my bra and threw them both in the garbage along with the skirt. Well at least that was the truth.

"What happened to your neck Trenice?" Jordan asked as I stood there naked.

"I dunno," I lied. "Le'me go look in the mirror," I said as I hurried into the bathroom. I thought I would have a minute to myself but Jordan was right behind me... "Hmm... it is red... probably from me leaning on the bags while I was on the train," I said as I kept looking in the mirror and massaging my neck...

"What were you doing on the train? I thought you were taking a cab home from White Plains?"

"I was, but it broke down," I lied.

"So why didn't you call another one?"

"I was tired of waiting and I just wanted to get home so when I saw the bus I just took it to the train station," I said as I turned on the shower.

"Why didn't you take a cab from there? Why'd you take the train all the way to 125th Street and then take another train to Yonkers when you could've just taken a cab from the train station? No wonder it took you so long to get home," he snapped.

"Didn't I tell you the fuckin' cab broke down?" I screamed. "I didn't want to take another fuckin' cab – I heard the train and I didn't feel like gettin' in line to wait for another fuckin' cab – I just wanted to get on the train and come home!" I cried as I turned and tried to get into the shower.

"Cumere Trenice," he said as he pulled me into his arms and held me as I continued to cry. "This isn't how our first night was supposed to be," he said as he stroked my hair.

"I'm sorry," I whispered.

"You don't have anything to be sorry about," he whispered as he started kissing me on my neck.

"Honey," I whispered as I gently pushed him away... "Let me get in the shower while you put the food away...I won't be long," I said as I ran down the hall towards the bedroom, stepped into the Jacuzzi, and turned on the shower.

"Ok – I'll be right back," he said.

I poured the entire bottle of shampoo on me and began scrubbing my hair vigoursly. "I gotta get him off me," I said as I continued to scrub my hair. "I gotta get him off me," I said as I grabbed the wash cloth and scrubbed myself so hard I was beet red from my face down to my feet.

"Guess who?" Jordan said as came up behind me and pulled me against him. "Trenice you're shaking – what's wrong?"

"Nothing honey," I lied. "You scared me that's all," I lied again.

"I missed you," he said.

"I missed you too," I said.

"I love you Trenice," he said as he picked my face up and kissed me.

"I love you too," I said in between kisses and tears.

"Let's go to bed," he said as he turned off the shower, stepped out of the Jacuzzi, and took my hand to help me out also.

"Ok," I said as he led me out of the bathroom and into the bedroom. When we got to the bedroom and got into bed he snuggled up behind me, pulled me close to him, and held me until he we both fell asleep.

We had been asleep for about 20 minutes when I woke up to go to the bathroom. As I was coming back into the bedroom I went to turn off the television when I heard the following:

"We interrupt our regularly scheduled programming to bring you this update. News 12 has just been informed that the Police and the FBI are looking for a serial rapist here in Westchester. So far, there have been rapes reported in Yonkers, Mt. Vernon, New Rochelle, Mamaroneck, Tarrytown, Irvington, Pelham, and Harrison. News 12 doesn't have a description of the rapist at this time; however, News 12 has been informed that the rapist is a cab driver and he was last seen in Harrison driving a 1984 Black Mercury Cougar. News 12 has also been informed by his latest victim that he carries a serrated hunter's knife. Residents here in Westchester are advised to stay indoors after 6pm unless you have a companion with you at all times. Residents in Westchester are also urged not to go into public garages unless they are well lit and under 24 hour surveillance. Stay tuned to News 12 for further updates. We now return to our regularly scheduled programming..."

Chapter 62

"Are you sure I can't call anyone for you Trenice?"

"Yes, I'm sure."

"Trenice, you really need to..."

"Thank you Dr. Campton," I cut in.

"Trenice I'll respect your privacy but..."

"Look doctor. – I know you mean well and I appreciate it – but the last thing I need right now is a fucking lecture!"

"Trenice!"

"I'm sorry – this isn't your fault – but what the hell am I gonna do?"

Dr. Campton could see I was losing it and when the nurse came in he shooed her out the door and gently placed his hand on my shoulder. When I flinched, he removed his hand, backed away from me, and said, "Trenice you can't keep going on like this. If you won't let me call anyone for you at least let me give you a mild sedative."

"You can't do that Dr. – I won't be able to explain the pills to Jordan."

"Trenice, you won't be able to explain anything to anybody if you try and keep this to yourself. Don't you think he'll understand?"

"I don't understand it myself doctor – how the hell am I supposed to make him understand?"

"Trenice it wasn't your fault – anyone with half a brain can see that..."

"I wish it were that simple doctor - after everything he went through with Rosalind – now here I am about to put him through the same shit!"

"Trenice this is not the same and you know it – what Rosalind did was conniving and malicious – she asked for it – you didn't ask to be raped."

"You know that and I know that – but how can I be sure he'll know that?"

"I wish I could answer that for you Trenice."

"I don't know what's worse – telling the man I love I could be carrying another man's baby or telling the man I love I could be HIV positive....Ohhhhhhhhh my God!" I screamed as Dr. Campton tried once again to comfort me as the nurse burst into the room...

"Is everything ok doctor? Can I get you something Trenice?"

"Yes – may I have some water please?"

"Sure thing Trenice – I'll be right back..."

"Trenice are you sure about this?"

"Well I knew in my heart I was pregnant – that's why when you asked me to have a chest x-ray I refused – I figured I was 1 month at the most – but once you said I was 2 months along that's when I knew…"

"Knew what Trenice?"

"Doctor, do you remember the last time I was in your office?

"Yes Trenice – it was to remove the cast off your leg."

"Well when I left your office I didn't go straight home – I went to the Food Emporium on Mamaroneck Avenue. I called Jordan and told him I was waiting on a cab. When the car pulled up and the driver said, "Taxi," – oh my God – how could I have been so stupid?!"

"What happened Trenice? Did he rape you? The cab driver?"

"I got in the cab and told him where I was going. He said he needed to stop to check the oil in his car. When he pulled up to his garage he said he needed to make a phone call and he would be right back. After I waited for about 10 minutes, I got out the car and went inside to use the bathroom…while I was on the toilet…he…he…he…"

"Dr. Campton held me as I cried on his shoulder.

"Oh my God Trenice – how have you been able to keep this all inside? How are you able to cope?"

"You haven't heard the worst of it doctor."

"Oh no – what else did he do Trenice?"

"It's what I did doctor."

"What do you mean Trenice? What could you do that's worse than gettin' raped?"

"Murder."

"Come again?"

"When he finished, he stepped away from me and turned his back and started fixin' his clothes…"

"Then what Trenice?"

"I picked up the cover off the back of the toilet and I killed that bastard!" I screamed.

"Are you sure Trenice?"

"Hell yea! I hit that bastard until the damn cover broke into pieces all over his body and the floor – he won't rape anyone else! After I made sure he was dead I went outside, grabbed my groceries, and took the bus home."

"How did you get away with this? I mean…shit – I don't know what I mean Trenice," he said as he hugged me.

"Did you see the news last night doctor?"

"I vaguely remember Trenice…"

"Have you seen the story on the serial rapist?"

"You gotta be fuckin' kidding me! That's the bastard that raped you?"

"That's the one."

"Trenice… don't take this the wrong way… but…what the fuck do you care? What jury would convict you? All his other victims will probably want to give you a fuckin' medal! I can't wait to tell my other patients that bastard is dead!"

"You can't do that doctor!"

"Hmmm…. I see you're your point – I guess they'll find out soon enough…why is the FBI still looking for him? Why would they continue to run this story on News 12…unless…oh my God – you didn't tell them did you?"

"No."

"Why Trenice?"

"I feel so stupid…"

"You have nothing to feel stupid about…"

"How can I be sure they'll believe me?"

"Why wouldn't they Trenice?"

"I don't know…I'm so confused…"

"Trenice - let your family help…"

"NO!! Don't you dare breathe a fucking word of this to anyone – especially my family!"

"Trenice I can't help you if you won't let me…"

"You wanna help me doctor?"

"You don't even have to ask Trenice…"

"How the fuck am I supposed to continue with this pregnancy knowing I could be carrying a rapists' child? How the fuck am I supposed to make Jordan understand why we both need to be tested for HIV again? Let's see – honey I didn't cheat on you but this baby may not be yours and there's a chance I could've infected you with HIV – think that'll go over well doctor?" I looked up and saw the nurse standing there in the doorway with my water. She had been listening the whole time.

"Ahem – here's your water Trenice."

"Thank you."

"Trenice?"

"Yes?" I asked sarcastically.

"I couldn't help but overhear…"

"Well can you help and fuckin' forget it?" I snapped.

"I'll never forget that bastard… or you….," she whispered with tears in her eyes. When Dr. Campton came back into the examination room and saw us hugging and crying, he assumed she was comforting me.

"Trenice?"

We both jumped and the water spilled on both of us...

"Shit! – I'm sorry," I said as I blotted us with paper towels.

"Thank you," she mouthed as she left the room.

"You're welcome," I mouthed back as Dr. Campton had his head in my chart.

"You'll need to come see me with Jordan in 3 months for the AIDS test."

"Oh my God – how am I gonna tell him?!"

"It won't be easy Trenice."

"What was I thinking? What if I've given him AIDS? I can't do this...I can't do this...I can't do this..."

When I came too, Jordan was sitting beside me holding my hand. "Hey Beautiful," he said as he gave me a kiss.

"How did you know I was here?"

"Dr. Campton called me."

"I had to call someone Trenice."

"That's ok Dr. Campton – I'm glad you called Jordan – now I can tell him the news." Dr. Campton looked at me strangely – complexed as well as confused.

"What news Trenice? Are you ok?"

"I'm pregnant."

"You're pregnant? So that's why you've been so sick!"

"Yea."

"I can't believe we're gonna have a baby! I love you soooooooo much!" he said as he grabbed me into a bear hug. "Why are you still lying down? Can she leave Dr.?"

"Yes but she needs to take care of herself."

"I'll make sure she does – believe me!"

"Jordan I need to speak to Trenice in private – can you wait outside?"

"Sure."

When he closed the door Dr. Campton said, "Trenice we can send some of your blood over to the lab and have it tested for HIV. If it comes back negative, I'll still need to see you and Jordan in another 3 months."

"Okay – but please don't send the results to my home – I'll pick them up here."

"Okay then. Make sure you see your gynecologist ASAP – you'll need to start taking some prenatal vitamins – and no more skipping meals – we can't have you having fainting spells – you gotta think about that little one you're carrying."

"Dr. I can't stop thinking about this little one I'm carrying…"

Jordan opened the door and said, "You coming Trenice?"

"On my way sweetie – thank you Dr."

"You're welcome Trenice."

Chapter 63

When we got home I called Char right away.

"Wow – 2 months huh?"

"Yea."

"So you happy?"

"Yea."

"You don't sound too happy – you ok Trenice?"

"Yea I'm ok Char – I'm just tired and hungry. I was kinda surprised though."

"The way you freaks been goin' at it? Why would you be surprised?"

"Cause I was on the pill."

"Oh damn – you one of the lucky ones."

"Yea I suppose so."

"Is Jordan happy?"

"Are you kidding? He's ecstatic – he's already called Jake and Rachel and he's on his way to tell his Mum-Mums now."

"I shoulda known..."

"I think the only reason I got to tell you myself is 'cause I got to the phone before he did!"

"Damn girl – he really wants this baby huh?"

"Yes indeed."

"Well at least he knows it's his baby and he won't have to worry about going through any of the shit he went through with Rosalind." I couldn't say anything. I just froze.

"Trenice? You still there?"

"Hello? Char?"

"Yea? Trenice?"

"Sorry girl – someone was at the door – I had to put the phone down a second," I lied.

"Girl when are you gonna start using the cordless phone?"

"I dunno Char."

"You sure you ok Trenice?"

"Yea – I'm gonna go lay down – I'll call you later ok?"

"Ok Trenice – take care – I love you."

"I love you too Char," I said trying not to choke. When I hung up the phone I sat at the table and sobbed.

I must have fallen asleep at the table 'cause Jordan woke me up. "Trenice, why didn't you go lay down?"

"Oh I guess I fell asleep – sorry."

"Who were you talking to?"

"Nobody."

"Oh so you just holding the phone for nothing then?"

"Oh sorry sweetie – I called Char to tell her the news. After I got off the phone I just laid my head down on the table…"

"Come here – I have something to show you…"

I followed Jordan into the living room and there were peach roses all over the living room. The lights were turned down and the flames from the peach candles cast a beautiful glow in the room. There was a platinum tray filled with fruit and cheese, a bottle of sparkling apple cider, and two champagne glasses. There were two boxes on the table – one was the size of a large gift box and the other was the size of a ring box.

"When did you do all this?"

"When I came in I saw you asleep at the table so I just set it up quickly, hoping you wouldn't wake up until I was finished." Jordan took me by the hand and led me to the sofa. When we both sat down he handed me the large box 1st. "Open this."

"Okay." When I opened the box there was a set of red satin pajamas for me, a set for him, and a tiny set for a newborn baby. "Oh Jordan – these are adorable!"

"I know it's too soon but I fell in love with them…just like I fell in love with you," he said as he pulled me into a kiss. "Trenice you're shaking – what's wrong?"

"Nothing's wrong."

"You sure?"

"I'm sure." He picked up the ring box and opened it.

"Trenice, will you marry me?"

"Yes Jordan – I'll marry you – I'll marry you!"

Jordan cried right along with me as he placed the ring on my finger. I had so many emotions going on I wasn't sure what I was feeling and to make matters worse, Jordan was holding up the newborn silk pajamas with one hand and had his arm wrapped around me with the other. Jordan poured two glasses of sparkling cider, and then picked up the tray of fruit and cheese and we fed each other until the tray was empty. Jordan picked up one glass of sparkling cider and handed me the other.

"Here's to us." He said as we both drank until the glasses were empty.

Chapter 64

The telephone startled us both. After we knocked it down and the receiver hit the floor, I grabbed it up...

"Hello?" I said out of breath.

"Damn girl – whatchall was doin'?"

"Oh hi Char."

"Y'all busy?"

"No-why?"

"So why you all out of breath?"

"I know you didn't call me to check my breathing!" I said laughing.

"Look – if you don't wanna talk I'll hang up..."

"Char wait a minute! What's wrong with you?"

"You actin' like you don't wanna talk n shit!"

"Who did it Char?"

"Did what?"

"Who made you so mad?"

"Nobody...nothing...forget it..."

"Char?"

"What!"

"C'mon Char...don't let me have to come over there and tickle you," I said laughing.

"Well, I wanted to come over but if y'all busy..."

"Girl if we was busy I wouldn't have answered the damn phone!" I hollered.

"Damn right," Jordan said in the background.

"Honey, Char wants to come over ok?"

"Sure. When's she comin'?"

"Now," she said and hung up.

"She's on her way now," I said as I put the phone down.

"Shall we get dressed?"

"For Char? Oh please," I laughed. When we heard the knock on the door we both jumped out of bed, scrambling to find our robes and pajamas.

"Trenice – it's me..."

"Be right there!" When I answered the door she came in, looked around at all the candles, the roses, the empty fruit tray, the empty bottle of sparkling cider, and the two glasses.

"See I knew y'all was busy."

"What are you talking about Char?"

"So how come you're not dressed?"

"Since when do we get dressed for you," I laughed.

"Whatchu tryina say?" she laughed as we hugged each other.

"Breakfast is ready ladies," Jordan interrupted.

"Aww honey, that is so sweet – thank you!"

"Yea – thank you honey," Char laughed.

We followed Jordan into the dining room and the table was a sight for hungry eyes. The eggs were scrambled with cheddar cheese to a nice bright yellow-orange color, along with turkey sausage, home fries with onions and peppers, fruit salad, buttermilk biscuits, orange juice, and coffee.

"Wow – what's the occasion?" Char asked.

"I just wanted to make you both breakfast," Jordan said as we all sat down.

"Y'all gonna tell me or what?" Jordan and I looked at each other as I pulled my right hand from underneath the table... "Oh my God! Y'all gettin' married?"

"Yes! Jordan proposed last night girl – 'member when I was on the phone with you?"

"Yea?"

"Girl, I fell asleep at the table."

"No you didn't – damn girl you was that tired?"

"Yea – Jordan came in, saw me sleep at the table, and set up the candles, the roses, the fruit tray, the sparkling apple cider – oh I gotta show you these – they are soooo cute," I said as I snatched her up from the table and took her by the hand into the living room to show her the baby silk pajamas.

"Oh my God – look at these! I'm so happy for you," Char said as she hugged us both.

"Let's go finish eating," Jordan said as we went back into the dining room. We sat, ate, and drank until we were stuffed. Jordan got up to clear the table and I snatched the back of his pajamas, turned him around, and gave him a long, passionate kiss.

"Um...y'all want me to leave?"

102

"No Char – don't be silly," Jordan said as he took the dishes into the kitchen.

"Char?"

"Yea Trenice?"

"What's wrong?" I asked.

"You two need to talk?" Jordan said.

"Yea, but can you stay Jordan?"

"Sure." We all sat down at the table and poured more coffee.

"I have a problem," she sighed.

"You do?" we both said in unison.

"Yea."

"What's wrong Char?"

"I think he went back to his wife." Jordan just turned his head to look out the window and threw up his hands without saying anything.

"Are you sure?" I asked.

"I don't know."

"Wait a minute Char..." Jordan said. "Either he did or he didn't."

"I haven't talked to him."

"So what makes you think we went back to his wife then?"

"He hasn't returned my calls – his pager is disconnected and I haven't seen him in about 2 months."

"Did you talk about any of this? Did he tell you he was going back to his wife?" Jordan asked.

"The last time I saw him was the day y'all left my house and you gave me that advice. I met with him and told him I didn't want to lose him – just like you said I should. He was soooo happy..."

"I bet he was!" Jordan said sarcastically, but Char didn't catch on.

"He told me we were gonna work things out but he needed to wait until he found out if his wife was pregnant first. He even told me he got a new job driving a taxi but I haven't seen him since!" Suddenly I got a sinking feeling in the pit of my stomach.

"Char?"

"Yea?"

"Did he drive a taxi in Yonkers?" "Please let her say yes, Lord..." I prayed to myself.

"I think I would have seen him if he drove a cab in Yonkers Trenice."

"Oh my God," I said as I ran to the bathroom to throw up...

"You alright Trenice?" Jordan asked.

"I think so," I lied. "I guess your little girl can only take one cup of coffee per hour," I laughed.

"A little girl? You sure about that?"

"I think so."

"Well there's a 50% chance you're wrong," Char laughed.

"So Char – where did he say he drove a taxi?" "Please don't say it, please don't say it, please don't say it," I said to myself.

"White Plains." I sat there and went numb as my palms got all sweaty.

"Trenice, you look pale – you sure you ok?"

"I'll be fine Char – what company did he work for?"

"Damn Trenice – what's with the twenty fuckin' questions?"

"Look Char – I'm just tryin' to help you," I lied.

"I got my cast off two months ago and I called a cab – besides I always take cabs home from White Plains – maybe I've seen him."

"I'm sorry Trenice. You probably haven't seen him though – it's a new company just starting out."

"God please let her be right," I prayed to myself.

"Char, I think you would know if he went back to his wife," Jordan said.

"You do?"

"Yea. He was straight with you about everything else – why wouldn't he be straight with you about that?"

"You right – thanks Jordan."

"Don't thank me yet Char."

"Why?"

"If you haven't seen or heard from him in 2 months his wife probably hasn't either. He may be missing."

"Oh my God – what makes you say that?"

"What other explanation is there?" he asked.

"No, No, No, No, No, No, No, No, NOOOOOOO!" I cried as I ran to the bathroom.

"Trenice – what's wrong?" Jordan asked.

"This little girl doin' flips making me nauseous," I lied.

"Maybe you need to lie down," Char said.

"Yea – maybe I do," I said as I came out the bathroom.

"Alright – I'ma go – see y'all later," she said as she hugged us both.

When she left Jordan asked, "Honey what's wrong?" God I wanted to tell him so bad.

"I'll be okay – I think I just over did it on the coffee and orange juice," I lied.

"You sure that's all? Something else is going on Trenice."

"I'm worried about Char," I lied.

"I knew it."

"What if he's dead?"

"You've been watching LAW & Order for too long," Jordan laughed.

"It does sound silly doesn't it?" I laughed.

"He probably moved on to another woman and left both their asses," he laughed again. "I think she's better off —now she can find her own man – hell she could even end up like us," he said as he pulled me into a kiss.

"That would be wonderful," I said as I kissed him back.

"So, how would you like to spend the rest of the day?" he asked while nibbling on my neck.

"Well, I wanna go to Grandma's house and tell her the good news," I said.

.

Chapter 65

When I got to Grandma's house I was greeted by my Mother, Aunt Trudy, and Sissy – as usual.

"Hi everybody!"

"Hi Trenice!" they all said in unison.

"So are ya or ain't cha?" Sissy asked.

"Huh?"

"Are you pregnant or not?"

"I'm fine Sissy – thanks for asking," I said sarcastically.

"Well excuse me!"

"As if there was an excuse for you," I mumbled.

"What?"

"Yes – I'm pregnant!" I yelled as I ran to hug my mother and my grandmother."

"Well congratulations – it only took a week for you to tell me," Grandma said.

"Oh – sorry Grandma – I was kinda busy."

"Too busy to pick up the damn phone?"

"I didn't want to call you – I wanted to come see you."

"Yea right."

"Cut it out Grandma," I said as I gave her a little tickle in her side.

"Stop it Trenice," she laughed. "Besides, Claire told me last week."

"I kinda figured that too."

"Oh you did?"

"Yea – Jordan made a beeline to his Mum-Mum's as soon as we left the hospital..." Shit! Oh well too late – it slipped out –

"Hospital? You alright?"

"Yea – I thought I had the flu with all this throwin' up, fever, loss of appetite..."

"You throwin' up already?" Aunt Trudy asked.

"Yea – I thought it was kinda early too until I found out I was two months pregnant."

"Damn Trenice – didn't you have the cast on your leg two month's ago?"

"Yea? So?"

"So I guess it didn't stop no show huh?" she said as they all bust out laughing.

"I guess it didn't."

"Trenice?"

"Yes Grandma?"

"What's wrong with your finger?"

"Nothing Grandma – why do you ask?" I said slyly. I knew what Grandma was talking about the whole time. Grandma came over to me and picked up my hand.

"Oh that..." I said

"Yea that!"

"Oh my God Trenice – Jordan proposed?"

"Yes – Jordan asked me to marry him and I said yes!"

"Oh my God – my baby's gettin' married!" my mother said with tears in her eyes as she grabbed me.

"Oh Claire, stop being so dramatic – she's not a baby," Grandma said as she playfully pushed my mother away from me and grabbed me into a hug.

"Grandma I know you not cryin!" I laughed.

"Oh girl hush up – I was just in the kitchen cutting onions," she said as she wiped her eyes.

"Yea right Ma!" Aunt Trudy and my mother said in unison as they both laughed.

"Be careful Trenice…"

"Huh?" I said, wondering what the hell Sissy was talking about.

"Marriage ain't all it's cracked up to be," Sissy said as she left out the door.

"What's her problem?" my mother asked.

"She and Cornell are separated. He left her for another woman," Aunt Trudy said.

"Damn – that's fucked up," my mother said.

"Well that explains her foul mood," Grandma said.

"She might be pregnant too – that's what's so fucked up," Aunt Trudy said.

"Oh my God, Oh my God, Oh my God, Oh my God, Oh my God!" kept running through my head. "This can't be happening, this can't be happening, this can't be happening, this can't be happening, this can't be happening," I said over and over as I shook my head back and forth…"

"Damn Trenice – what's wrong with you?" Aunt Trudy asked.

"Nothing...I mean...damn – I didn't even know she was married!"

"Her husband left her a long time ago. He just filed for a legal separation a few month's ago..."

"No, no, no, no, no, no, no, no, no!" I yelled.

"Trenice – what is wrong with you?" Grandma yelled.

"Nothing – I just can't believe it – to look at Sissy you would never know..."

"Well make sure you keep it that way – don't go runnin' your mouth." Aunt Trudy said.

"Oh like she does?" I said sarcastically.

"Don't start that shit you two," Grandma said.

"Just because she's mean doesn't mean I have to be, Aunt Trudy."

"So watchu sayin'?"

"I'm sayin' I'm happy Jordan and I are gettin' married. I didn't come over here to rub anything in Sissy's face. You haven't even congratulated me – you too busy worryin' if I'm gonna tell Sissy's business!"

"Ma I gotta go – see ya later," she said as she slammed the door.

"I swear – you two get on my fuckin' nerves," Grandma said.

"That not right Grandma. She can say whatever she wants and she expects me not to say anything 'cause she's my aunt..."

"I don't care who's right or wrong Trenice – it just gets on my fuckin' nerves – that's all."

"No disrespect Grandma, but it gets on my fuckin' nerves too..."

"Watch your mouth Trenice..." my mother said.

"See what I mean? Bye Grandma," I said as I slammed the door on my way out.

"Trenice get back here!" my mother yelled after me but I made a beeline down the stairs and out the building. As luck would have it I ran smack into Sissy and Aunt Trudy.

"Where you goin' Trenice? You just got here," Sissy said.

"I'm going home Sissy. I'm going home!"

Chapter 66

"I don't fuckin' believe this shit!" I said as I slammed my keys on the table.

"Hey Beautiful," Jordan said as he pulled me into a kiss.

"Hey," I said with my head down.

"What's wrong? Didn't you tell them we're gettin' married?"

"Yea."

"They weren't too happy?"

"They were ecstatic – at least my mother and grandmother were..."

"Fuckin' Trudy right?"

"That's only part of it..."

"Damn Trenice – what the fuck happened!"

"You're not going to believe this... you better sit down..."

"Okay."

"Well, first thing I get in the house, Sissy askin', "Are you or ain't cha? – just like that!"

"What is wrong with her?"

"I'm gettin' to it…"

"Okay, okay…"

"So I said Yes – I'm pregnant, then Grandma notices the ring so then I tell them you asked me to marry you – my mother and grandma were all excited – then – out of nowhere – Sissy tells me be careful 'cause marriage ain't all it's cracked up to be!"

"Get the fuck outta here!"

"Yea! Then when she leaves Aunt Trudy tells us…"

"What Trenice – what!"

"She tells us Sissy's husband left her for another woman!"

"So? What the fuck does that have to do with you?"

"She says he left her a long time ago and he filed for a legal separation about 6 months ago."

"Are you fuckin' kidding me?"

"Nope. And, she says Sissy thinks she's pregnant."

"You must have been shocked!"

"I was! They all askin' me what's wrong so I had to play it off like I was feelin' sorry for her 'n shit…"

"I bet…if they only knew…"

"So I'm like damn – to look at Sissy you would never know, so Aunt Trudy gonna say keep it that way and don't be runnin' my mouth!"

"Fuckin' bitch!"

"Exactly!" So I said I don't have to be mean just 'cause she's mean – then I said you ain't even congratulate me 'cause you so worried about me tellin' Sissy's business!"

"Oh I know she got mad then," Jordan laughed.

"Yea, well she ain't the only one..."

"Really?"

"Yea! She gonna get up and slam the door and Grandma gonna tell me we get on her fuckin' nerves!"

"Get the fuck outta here!"

"So I told Grandma that ain't right – she say what she wanna say and she think I ain't gonna say nothing 'cause she my Aunt – then Grandma gonna say she don't care who's right or wrong – it just gets on her fuckin' nerves!"

"Damn!"

"So I said it gets on my fuckin' nerves too!"

"No you didn't!"

"Yes I did! So my mother tells me watch my mouth – so I got up and slammed the door!"

"Damn!"

"Then my mother gonna holla at me to get back there – like I was really goin' back upstairs!"

"I don't believe this shit!"

"Oh it gets better! I ran right into Sissy and Aunt Trudy when I got outside!"

"What they say?"

"Aunt Trudy ain't say shit but Sissy gonna ask me where I'm goin' 'cause I just got there..."

"Oh so now you gotta explain shit to her too?" Jordan laughed.

"I guess so – so I did explain it – I told her I was goin' home! I'm so fuckin' mad!"

"Calm down Trenice – you're home now," Jordan said as he kissed my neck. I wrapped my arms around him, pulled him close, and said,

"Damn right I'm home! And I don't have to put up with that shit anymore!"

"So you gonna tell Char?"

"Hell no! I wish Aunt Trudy never told me!"

"Why did she tell you anyway?"

"Who knows? Then she gonna tell me don't run my mouth – I wonder if she would like it if I told Sissy she was runnin' her business...I should go right back over there and..."

"No you shouldn't Trenice. Just let it go," he said as he rubbed my shoulders and back.

"You're right – besides what good would it do? I have better things to focus on than Cornell and Sissy."

"Who?!" Jordan jumped up so fast he scared me.

"Cornell. Why?"

"Trenice, Cornell didn't leave Sissy. Not by choice anyway."

"What are you talking about?"

"Trenice, Cornell was in prison for the last 12 years for rape."

"How do you know that?"

"Me, Jake, Cain, William, and Cornell used to ball back in the day. One night after the game was finished we all lookin' around for Cornell. Then we heard screamin' comin' from behind the baseball field so we ran over there..."

"Oh my God! You saw him?"

"Yea. That was some fucked up shit too. Cain saw him first. When me, Jake, and William got over there he was still on top of the girl. Cain snatched him up off the girl and broke his jaw. Me, Jake, and

William commenced to bustin' his ass! The girl ran and so did we when we heard the cops comin'."

"Y'all just left him there?"

"Damn right!"

"So what happened?"

"The cops took him to the hospital."

"So how he wind up in Jail?"

"The girl pressed charges. She said some guys helped her get away but they had his DNA so they didn't bother lookin' for us – besides – she couldn't tell them what we looked like anyway – she was to focused on what Cornell looked like."

"I'm glad they got his ass. Now I'm really worried about Char."

"I still can't believe Char is seeing Cornell, Cornell is married to Sissy, and Sissy might be pregnant. I wonder if Char knows who Cornell's wife is."

"Probably not. Remember – he don't want nobody to know nothing 'till his divorce is final?"

"Damn! Well I hope Char is safe."

"Maybe she is Jordan."

"What makes you so sure Trenice?"

"Well she's been coming over here talking to us. She doesn't seem to be in danger. Seems like the only thing she's worried about is whether he's going back to his wife."

"True."

"I'll ask her."

"Oh so you gonna tell her you know?"

"Hell no! I'm just gonna ask her if she ever met his wife."

"You gonna ask her his name?"

"No she's too smart for that – remember the swing?"

"How could I forget," he laughed.

Chapter 67

I woke up earlier than usual. I couldn't go back to sleep so I turned on News 12. I went into the kitchen to make myself a cup of coffee and when I came back into the dining room, I dropped the cup on the table, spilling coffee all over the place, damn near cutting myself on the pieces as Jordan came flying into the dining room...

"Damn Trenice – you ok?" Jordan asked as he started to clean up the broken pieces."

"Yes I'm ok," I said as I continued to watch News 12:

"Police and the FBI are still looking for the serial rapist..."

"What are you lookin' at Trenice?" Jordan asked as he looked towards the television. We were both in shock as News 12 continued:

"We now have a description of the serial rapist as described by his latest victim…"

"Oh my God – Cornell!" Jordan yelled.

"Oh my God, Oh my God, Oh my God, Oh my God, Oh my God!" I yelled.

"Damn – I wonder if Char's seen this?" Jordan said. I couldn't believe I was looking at the man that raped me. The man Jordan played ball with. The man Sissy was married to. The man Char was in love with. The man whose child I may be carrying. The man I murdered…

"He was last seen in White Plains, NY over 2 months ago. He was last seen driving a 1984 Black Mercury Cougar. No recent rapes have been reported; however, this man is considered armed and extremely dangerous. Police and the FBI have been ordered to shoot on site. Residents here in Westchester are advised to stay indoors after 6pm unless you have a companion with you at all times. Residents in Westchester are also urged not to go into public garages unless they are well lit and under 24 hour surveillance. Stay tuned to News 12 for further updates. We now return to our regularly scheduled programming…"

"Trenice! Trenice! Trenice wake up!" Jordan yelled as he shook me.

"What happened?"

"You fainted. You ok?" I started to cry uncontrollably. "Oh my God Trenice – you're scaring me…" he said as he rocked me back and forth. "Don't cry baby – please don't cry," he said as he started crying with me.

"Honey, don't cry," I said as I continued crying myself."

"I can't stand to see you hurting like this Trenice – please don't cry anymore," he said as he continued crying with me..."

"Oh my God – what happened – Trenice you ok? – Why y'all cryin'? Did somebody die?"

"Char whatchu doin' here?" we asked in unison.

"How'd you get in here anyway?" Jordan asked.

"Trenice gave me the key in case of emergency. I heard y'all in here and it sounded like something broke so I used the key to make sure everything was ok."

"I'm glad you did Char," I said.

"So why didn't you answer the door?"

"We didn't hear you Char. Trenice dropped her cup of coffee and damn near cut herself."

"So why y'all cryin?"

"He's cryin 'cause he's worried about me."

"Why?"

"Cause I fainted."

"Why you fainted?"

"Char you haven't seen News 12 have you?"

"No – what's goin' on y'all – now I wanna cry..."

"You probably will," I said as she sat at the table and News 12 ran the story again."

"Oh God – Nooooooooooooooooo!" Char yelled as she broke down crying. "I can't believe it – how could he do this Trenice?"

"I don't know Char," I said as we hugged each other crying.

"I love him sooo much – how could he do this – why, why, why, why, why, why?"

120

"Ok that's it – we're turning off this damn television and y'all gonna stop cryin' over that bastard!" Jordan yelled as he hugged us both with tears in his eyes.

"Ain't this a bitch – my best friend cryin' and her man cryin' too – I don't deserve y'all," Char said as she cried some more. "I shoulda listened to y'all – I was so stupid!"

"Char you had no idea what he was capable of. If I knew you was seein' Cornell from the beginning I would've warned you to stay the hell away from him in the first place."

"Whatchu mean?" She jerked around so fast she went from hurt to angry in 2 seconds. "How you know Cornell?"

"We used to ball back in the day. He spent 12 years in jail for rape."

"Oh my   God – I can't believe I was in love with him," Char said as she started crying again."

"Enough of this shit! That bastard doesn't deserve any more tears from any of us! Char be glad you got away before he hurt you too."

"All those women – and what about the women that didn't report it? Trenice why you lookin' at me like that? Trenice?"

"Huh? Oh – I'm just as shocked as you Char – that's all."

"I know that mothafucka better not show his face now 'cause he's a fuckin' dead man!"

"You got that right," I said. If Char only knew how right she was...

"Trenice?"

"Yea?" "

Y'all was cryin before I got in here..."

"Yea..."

"So how did you know I was gonna be upset? And why did you tell me I was gonna start cryin' when I saw News 12?"

"I told you she was too smart to try and pull anything over her eyes Jordan."

"Tell her Trenice."

"Tell me what? Oh my God – what the fuck is goin' on?"

"Char I wish you didn't have to hear this from me..."

"Y'all are really scarin' me – just say it..." she said as she started cryin again.

"Sit down Char."

"Ok – can I have some water please?"

"Ok – I'll be right back – tell her Trenice..." Jordan said as he went into the kitchen to get Char some water.

"Ok here goes...I went to Grandma's to tell them the good news..."

"Good news?"

"Yea – you know – me being pregnant and we gettin' married..."

"Oh ok..."

"So Sissy tells me be careful 'cause marriage ain't all it's cracked up to be..."

"Ok..."

"So when she leaves, my mother asked what her problem was..."

"Ok..."

"So Aunt Trudy tells us that her husband left her for another woman..."

"Trenice I know you not telling me..."

"Let me finish Char..."

"Ok go 'head..."

"So Aunt Trudy says he filed for divorce a few months ago and Sissy thinks she's pregnant." Char just sat there and didn't say a word. "Char? Did you hear me?"

"Yea I heard you – but how you know it's Cornell?"

"Aunt Trudy said her husband's name was Cornell Char. We even got in a big blow up over it..."

"Oh my God – please tell me you didn't tell that bitch I was fuckin' her friends husband!"

"Char!"

"I'm sorry, I'm sorry..."

"So we got in a big blow up 'cause Aunt Trudy gonna tell me don't be runnin' my mouth and Grandma gonna tell me we both get on her fuckin' nerves..."

"What?!"

"Yea girl! So I came home and I'm tellin' Jordan what happened n shit and he tells me he used to ball with Cornell back in the day."

"When you first came over here and told us you hadn't heard from him in about 2 months, I told Trenice he probably picked up with another woman and you were better off," Jordan said as he came back into the dining room with a pitcher of water with ice and 3 glasses.

"Shit – I wish he had – that would'a been better than this shit," she said as she shook her head with tears in her eyes.

"Don't you start cryin' over that bastard again Char," Jordan said.

"Say what you want about him Jordan but God help me, I loved him, I loved him, I loved him," she said as she cried on my shoulder.

"I know you did Char and I'm sorry – but he didn't deserve your love and he doesn't deserve your pity..."

"I know but I can't help how I feel."

"You gonna tell the police?" Jordan asked.

"Hell no – they not gettin' shit from me – I hope they fry his ass!" she yelled as she wiped her eyes.

Chapter 68

I hadn't heard from Char all week. I wasn't surprised but I was kinda worried about her. I wished I could talk to Jordan about it - I'd been lying for so long I wouldn't even know where to begin. I wished I could talk to Char about it but how could I explain to my best friend that I was one of Cornell's victims? Shit – bad enough his wife thinks she's pregnant – what about me?

"Oh my God, Oh my God Oh my God Oh my God Oh my God!" I screamed as I thought about me and Sissy carrying that monster's child. "God I wish I had someone to talk to," I said out loud.

"Your prayers have been answered," Grandma said as she walked into the living room and plopped down beside me on the sofa.

"Grandma!" I hugged her so tight she said,

"Trenice – I can't breathe!"

"Oh – sorry Grandma. How'd you get in?"

"Jordan let me in on the way out."

"Oh." She followed me to the dining room and sat down at the table as I turned on News 12. I peeked at the television and saw the usual – News, Sports, Schools, and Weather. "Whew!" I sighed to myself. "Grandma I'ma go in the kitchen and make some coffee ok?"

"I'll come keep you company."

"I'd like that."

"You ok Trenice?"

"Sure."

"Something's up with you Trenice."

"I'm ok Grandma – really."

"Trenice I love you but right now I wanna choke the shit out of you!"

"Why Grandma?"

"Maybe If I choke you 'till you can't breathe, you'll tell me what's bothering you. And don't try and tell me you all worried about Sissy either 'cause I know better.

"I am kinda worried about Sissy Grandma."

"Cut the shit Trenice."

"Grandma!"

"Okay, okay – what?"

"Well – weren't you surprised?"

"Yea? So?"

"Well, to be honest I always thought Sissy was a nosy mean-spirited miserable bitch!"

"Trenice!"

"Well I did Grandma...until after Aunt Trudy said what she said."

"Whada you mean?"

"I'm just sayin' I understand her a little bit – I mean here I am having a baby, all excited about gettin' married and she goin' through all that – if it was me and Jordan I'd be a mean bitch too."

"I guess."

I made the coffee and Grandma followed me to the dining room table. When we sat down she took my hand. "Trenice what's really goin' on? I sense a sadness coming from you – are you happy? Is this what you really want?"

"Yes Grandma – I'm happy – I really love Jordan – I really wanna marry him – I really wanna have his child…" All of a sudden – out of nowhere, I burst into tears. Grandma didn't say anything – she just got up, put her arms around me, and let my cry.

"Remember I used to hold you like this and let you cry when you had a bad day in school?"

"Uh huh."

"Then you'd get up, go outside, and play like nothing ever happened."

"I remember," I laughed, "But I can't go outside and play now Grandma."

"Why can't you?"

"Huh?"

"Go on – get dressed – let's go outside and play!"

"Ok Grandma – I'll be right back," I said as I ran into the bathroom, took the quickest shower on record, threw on some jeans, a sweatshirt, and some sneakers, pulled my hair back in a ponytail, and came back into the living room.

"I haven't seen you look like that in a long time Trenice."

"Is that a good thing?"

"That's a great thing."

"So where we goin' Grandma?"

"To the park – where else?" she laughed.

When we got outside we walked to Carvel and stopped for ice cream.

"Grandma, remember I used to bring you home thiny-thin ice cream every payday?"

"I remember Trenice."

When we got outside we walked to Pelton Field and sat down on the bench, eating our ice cream as we watched the children play in the sand box. Grandma watched me as I watched the children go up the ladder, down the sliding board, and into the pile of sand below. I knew she wasn't going to let me off the hook so I set her up...

"Grandma?"

"Yes Trenice?"

"What if I'm not a good mother?"

"Is that what's been bothering you?"

"Yea," I lied.

"Why would you think you're not going to be a good mother?"

"Well Grandma..."

"Yea?"

"Look at my mother."

"Trenice, Claire did the best she could..."

"I know she did Grandma but look what she went through – and look at Shaliyah and Me..."

"Trenice you're a wonderful mother."

"And you know this because...?"

"Trenice – remember that bird?"

I bust out laughing.

"Remember how you put a splint on the wing and you cried when it flew away?"

128

"Yea I do," I laughed.

"And let's not forget that damn dog!" she laughed.

"Oh brother – how could I forget? I had to clean up behind that damn dog constantly – all that diarrhea – remember when I wrapped it in a towel and put it in the hamper so I could take it to the shelter?" I laughed.

"Of course I remember Trenice."

"Grandma?"

"Yes Trenice?"

"I feel a lot better now," I lied.

"I feel better too Trenice – I'm glad Jordan called me..."

"Jordan called you?"

"Yes he did. He says you haven't been sleeping too good – you toss and turn all night."

"I haven't been sleeping all that great..."

"You have nightmares Trenice?"

"Not really – why?"

"Jordan says sometimes you cry in your sleep."

"That's true – he did have to wake me up a couple of times."

"Why Trenice?

"Well...I had this dream that someone was after me," I lied.

"Yea? What happened?"

"I ran and ran but he cornered me...so I started screaming...his hand was this close to my neck and right before he could touch me, Jordan woke me up."

"How long have you been having that dream?"

"I don't have them anymore since Jordan leaves the TV on the Cartoon Network when we go to bed," I lied.

"The Cartoon Network?"

"Yea – we put the TV on the timer and Jordan likes to watch those science fiction movies – I think I was having those nightmares 'cause I would fall asleep while he was watching them," I lied.

Grandma bust out laughing. "Just like when you were little," she said as she hugged me. I hugged her back and we just sat there watching the children play until their parents came to pick them up one by one by one. Then we got up and headed back home.

When we got back home Jordan was there.

"Hi Honey."

"Hey Beautiful," he said as he pulled me into a kiss. "Hi Miss Gladys," he said as he snatched her into a bear hug.

"I swear – between you and Trenice y'all gonna squeeze the breath outta me!" she laughed as he put her down.

"Thank you Honey."

"You're welcome."

"Well I gotta get home so I'ma go on – don't forget my number Trenice," she said as we hugged each other.

"I won't Grandma."

"I love you."

"I love you too."

As she left Jordan said, "I think you really needed your Grandma Trenice."

"I did Jordan. I feel much better."

I did feel a little better after spending the day with Grandma but this whole situation was wearing me down. I've told so many lies I'm actually starting to believe some of them. How in the hell am I gonna make it for another 6 months? What am I gonna do after the baby's born? Oh my God – what if me and Sissy end up in the delivery room at the same time?

"Trenice? Trenice? Trenice!"

"Huh?" I answered as Jordan interrupted my thoughts...

"What the fuck is this?" he said as he threw the letter on the table.

"Son of a bitch!" I yelled. "I told them not to send this to my house – I don't fuckin' believe this!

"What the fuck is goin' on Trenice?"

"Honey...I can explain..."

"We both got tested a long time ago – why would you need to get tested again unless..."

"Honey...I can explain..."

"You fuckin' cheatin' on me?"

"Noooo!" I jumped up and ran to the door...
"Who is it?"

"It's me Trenice – open the door!" I scrambled to open the door as Jordan came up behind me...

"So what the fuck is goin' on then Trenice?"

"What's wrong with you – get away from her!" Char yelled as she pushed Jordan away from me...

"Char – it's okay..."

"No the fuck it's not ok – I heard y'all in the hallway..."

"Char – mind your fuckin' business!" Jordan yelled as he came towards me again with the paper in his hand...

"What the fuck is this Trenice? If you not cheatin' on me why didn't you want them to send this to the house!?"

"Jordan back up off her and leave her alone!" Char yelled.

"Char – it's ok – I'm alright – honey…I can explain…"

"No you're not – what the fuck is goin' on with you two?"

"Since you wanna be all up in it maybe you can explain this shit!" he yelled as he threw the paper at her. Char picked up the paper and read it aloud:

"We are writing to inform you we have received your test results. Your HIV test is negative. An appointment has been scheduled for you for 3 months from today…" she stopped reading…

"Well Trenice? You said you can explain it right? So explain why – if we both got tested long before you got pregnant – why was it necessary for you to get tested again now that you're pregnant? And why do they need to run another test on you in 3 months? The only time I know they do HIV tests on pregnant women is if somebody's positive or the baby's positive and I know damn well…wait a minute - whose baby is it Trenice??? Well???"

"I don't know," I whispered.

"Where you goin' Jordan? She said she can explain…"

"You know what? Right about now I gotta get up outta here before I strangle that bitch!" he yelled as he slammed the door…

"This is all my fault," I cried as Char hugged me. "I should've told him – I should've told him…"

"Told him what Trenice?"

"I never should've lied to him…"

"Trenice – what did you lie about?"

"Dr. Campton warned me this would happen but I didn't listen…"

"Trenice - what are you talking about?"

"After everything Rosalind put him through – how could I do this to him?"

"What did you do Trenice?"

"Oh God!" I screamed as I double over in pain.

"Trenice – what's wrong?"

"Oh God – it hurts!"

"Trenice you're bleeding – I'm calling an ambulance!" Char grabbed my keys off the table and sat back down beside me. Do you want me to call anyone when we get to the hospital?"

"Yea – call my Grandma."

"Ok. Do you know where Jordan is?"

"He's at Jake and Rachel's house…ugh!" I cried as I double over in pain again. Char got up to open the door for the paramedics and I nearly collapsed as they put me on the stretcher and put me in the ambulance.

"Where's your doctor?" the paramedic asked. "White Plain's Hospital – Ugh!"

"We're taking you to the nearest hospital – St. John's.

"Char?"

"Yes Trenice?"

"Please don't leave me…"

"I won't Trenice – I promise."

Chapter 69

When we got to the hospital I was taken to the back right away. I knew the news wouldn't be good once they hooked me up to the fetal monitor and the needles didn't move. They tried and tried to find my baby's heart beat to no avail.

"I'm sorry Trenice," the doctor said as Char and I hugged each other crying uncontrollably. "We'll need to examine you to make sure there's no remaining tissue. I lay there numb as Char held my hand while the doctor examined me.

When the nurse hooked me up to an IV I asked, "What's wrong?"

"It looks like you may have some blockage – we'll have to do a D & C..."

"I just had a miscarriage and now I have to have an abortion?"

"No no Trenice – you may have some scar tissue – we need to remove it asap – we can't risk you gettin' an infection – you could end up losing your fallopian tube all together – then your chances of gettin' pregnant again will be slim to none." That went through me like a knife.

"Oh my God – what if I can't ever give Jordan a child?" I screamed...

"Nurse – get her a sedative...

When I woke up Char was holding my hand. "Welcome back."

"What time is it Char?"

"It's 6pm."

"Oh my God – we've been here all day?"

"Yep."

"Did you call my Grandma?"

"Yea – they on their way."

"Oh boy – I hope the doctor's ready – remember the last time we all wound up in the hospital?"

"Yea."

"Trenice?"

"Yea?"

"Can I ask you something?"

"Ok," I said as if I had a choice...

"You never cheated on Jordan right?"

"No." I said.

"Well..."

"Yea Char?"

"I'm confused..."

"So am I Char." Just then my grandmother, my mother, Miss April, Miss June, Jake, Rachel, and all my brothers and sisters came into the room.

"There's too many people in here," the nurse said – "I'm gonna have to ask you all to go back downstairs – visitors are only allowed two at a time!"

"Nurse?"

"Yes?" she said hastily.

"Can you please let them stay for a few minutes? I promise I'll send them downstairs..."

"Alright – 10 minutes – but that's it – next thing you knew everybody will expect me to do them a favor..."

I saw Grandma gettin' up to go towards her so I said quickly, "Thank you nurse."

When she left Grandma said, "I was gettin' ready to tell that bitch something."

"I know you were," I said as we all laughed.

"Trenice?"

"Yes Shaliyah?"

"Where's Jordan?" Everyone looked at Shaliyah then back at me.

"He's on his way – he'll probably be here in another hour or so," Jake said.

"Did Jordan hurt you Trenice?"

"No Shaliyah – of course not – why would you think that?"

"Daddy hit Mommy one time and Mommy was in the hospital," she said. Everyone just sat there quiet.

"Shaliyah – Jordan didn't hurt me – I promise."

"But Mommy said we had to come to the hospital 'cause you got hurt - so who hurt you?"

"Nobody hurt me Shaliyah – I'm here because I'm sick."

"Oh."

"Trenice?"

"Yes Shaliyah?"

"When you go home can I come to your house?"

"Sure."

"Ok."

Just then the 'Warden' came back into the room.

"I know – they gotta leave right?"

"No – I just came to check your blood pressure – but be careful – if security catches you all in here they'll ask you to leave."

"Ok – thank you nurse."

"Well we might as well get going," My mother said as she gave me a hug. Everyone else followed with hugs and kisses. As they were leaving I called Jake back into the room.

"He's not coming is he?" Jake didn't answer me directly – he just shook his head no.

"Well, I'ma let you get some sleep Trenice," Char said as she got up.

"Thanks for everything Char. I love you."

"I love you too Trenice."

"See you tomorrow Char?"

"See you tomorrow Trenice."

I sat there flicking the channels 'round and 'round for a few minutes, then I grabbed the pen and paper out the drawer and started writing:

So Lost Without You Babe

As I sit here alone (so lost without you babe).
I 'm not sure what went wrong (so lost without you babe)
I just can't understand (so lost without you babe).
how things got out of hand (so lost without you babe).

I'm so numb I don't feel - can't accept this is real
I don't know how to stand - without you I don't know
who I am...

And I - I feel like my well has run dry
And I have such pain that I can't even cry
And I can't live without you in my life -

Can't you see you're the best part of me?

I don't sleep, I can't eat (so lost without you babe).
Still feel you in my dreams (so lost without you babe).
Walk around in a daze (so lost without you babe).
when I hear love songs play (so lost without you babe).

I'm so numb I don't feel - can't accept this is real.
I don't know how to stand - without you I don't know
who I am...

And I - I feel like my well has run dry
And I have such pain that I can't even cry
And I can't live without you in my life

Can't you see you're the best part of me?

I put the song in the drawer and turn on News 12:
        "We interrupt our regularly scheduled
programming to bring you this update. There has just
been an explosion in White Plains at the Getty
Station on Mamaroneck Avenue. Firefighters have
yet to determine the cause of the explosion; however,
they have recovered two bodies from the garage. Stay
tuned to News 12 for further updates."

I lay there in shock as I saw the garage where I was raped going up in flames. "Two bodies have been recovered from the garage..." kept playing over and over in my head.

"Trenice."

"Am I dreaming?"

"No you're not dreaming – I'm here," Jordan said as he climbed into the bed and cradled me in his arms. I cried and cried until I couldn't cry anymore. Jordan picked my chin up, kissed my lips and my eyes, and then he held my face in his hands and said, "Trenice, why didn't you tell me? Don't you know much I love you?"

"You know?"

"I know you were raped Trenice."

"But how..."

"When I left the house this morning I went to Jake and Rachel's house."

"I know..."

"I told them what you said – about the baby..."

"I'm sorry..."

"Shhhhh...don't cry..."

"But Jordan..."

"Let me finish..."

"Ok."

"I told them what happened and they said I should go see Dr. Campton so I called his office. They wouldn't tell me anything over the phone so I went up there in person."

"Oh God!" I screamed.

"Calm down Trenice – its ok – let me finish..."

"Ok."

"So I told them it was an emergency and I needed to see Dr. Campton right away to take another HIV test..."

"Ok."

"Once I got in to see the doctor I told him what happened – and guess what he said?"

"What?"

"He said he was gonna fire that bitch receptionist 'cause he left a note in your chart giving explicit instructions that you were to be called to the office and that the letter was not to be sent to the house!"

"That's what the fuck she gets – nasty bitch!"

"That's when I knew something was goin' on, so I asked the doctor point-blank – and he still wouldn't tell me anything – he said I had to ask you."

"Oh God – Jordan, I'm so sorry...I can explain..."

Jordan grabbed me and kissed me fully in the lips...

"What was that for?"

"'It's the only way I know to keep you from talking,' he laughed.

"Ok – I'm sorry," I laughed. "Go 'head."

"So I told him you were in the hospital and you had a miscarriage and that's when he told me you were raped." We sat there holding each other while News 12 ran the news from earlier in the day... "Trenice?"

"Yes?"

"I need you to make me a promise..."

"Ok."

"No more secrets – ok?" I started crying again... "Trenice, its ok – now I know..."

"No you don't," I whispered.

"What do you mean?"

"I need to tell you what happened..."

"Trenice I don't need to know what happened..."

"Yes you do..."

"Trenice, its ok..."

"No it isn't!" I yelled.

"Calm down Trenice – please calm down," he said as he stroked my hair.

"I can't promise you no more secrets if I'm still keeping secrets from you," I whispered.

"Oh my God Trenice – what happened?" Just then the 'Warden' came into the room...

"Excuse me – visiting hours are over..."

"My husband just got here – can he stay for a little while? Please?"

"Your husband? Well why didn't you say so? Of course he can stay!" she said as she closed the door.

"That sounds good," Jordan said as he kissed my neck..."

"Honey I need you to listen to me ok?"

"Ok – I'm listening," he said as he sat on the edge of the bed.

"Remember when I went to get the cast off?

"Yes – that was nearly 3 months ago..."

"Well after I got the cast off, I went to the Food Emporium for dinner – I should've come straight home and gone to Shoprite..." I said as I started crying again...

"Trenice you don't have to tell me anymore..."

"Yes I do!" I yelled.

"Ok, ok, ok – go 'head..."

"Remember when I called you from the Food Emporium?"

"Yea."

"Well – after I went shopping – I called you to tell you I was in the cab and he had to stop for gas and check the engine..."

"Yea – I remember..."

"When the car pulled up the security guard told me my cab was there so I got in - oh my God – how could I have been so stupid?!"

"What happened Trenice?"

"I got in the cab and told him where I was going. He said he needed to stop for gas and to check the engine. After he got the gas and checked under the hood he went inside the station. After I waited for about 10 minutes, I got out the car and went inside to use the bathroom...while I was on the toilet...he...he...he..."

"I'll fuckin' kill him! I'll fuckin' kill him! – You reported it right? Have they caught the bastard yet? What the fuck does he look like? Is he from around here? I better not see his ass around here or..."

"Jordan listen!"

"Ok – go 'head."

"He put a knife to my throat and told me to stand up..."

"Stop it! - I don't wanna hear it! – Just stop it!" Jordan cried as he grabbed me and squeezed me so tight I could hardly breathe..."

"I'm sorry but I need to..."

"No the fuck you don't Trenice! – I don't need to hear anymore..."

"I can't do this anymore – I can't stop the screaming in my head – the nightmares won't go away …"

"Let me help you Trenice, let me help you…"

"You wanna help me?"

"I'll do anything to take this pain away from you Trenice…"

"Then let me get this out – let me tell you what happened!" I yelled.

"Ok – go 'head."

"When he finished, he stepped away from me and turned his back and started fixin' his clothes…"

"Then what Trenice?"

"I picked up the cover off the back of the toilet and I killed him…" I whispered.

"You did what?"

"I killed him."

"Are you sure Trenice?"

"Oh yea! I hit him over and over and over until the cover broke into pieces all over his body and the floor – he won't rape anyone else!"

"Damn right – 'cause if you didn't kill his ass I would have!"

"After I made sure he was dead I went outside, grabbed my groceries, and took the bus to the Trans Center, and took Metro North home."

"That's why you didn't want me to touch you – I was wondering why you kept pushing me away…"

"I needed to get in the shower and wash him off of me…"

"Oh my God – I can't believe you were going through all this… I'm sorry… Does anybody else besides Dr. Campton know?"

"I looked up and saw the nurse standing there in the doorway - she had been listening the whole time."

"Damn! What she say?"

"She said I couldn't help but overhear..., so I said, well can you help and fuckin' forget it, then she tells me she'll never forget that bastard or me!"

"She was raped too? By the same man that raped you?"

"Yea."

"Well at least it's all out now..."

"No it isn't."

"Oh my God! – I'm afraid to ask – what else?"

"And I'm afraid to tell you..."

"My God Trenice – I'm surprised you haven't had a nervous breakdown..."

"Let me finish Honey..."

"Ok – go 'head."

"Remember when Char came over telling us she hadn't heard from her friend in about 2 months?"

"Yea?"

"Remember you said he was probably missing?"

"Yea?"

"Remember when I asked you what if he's dead?"

"Yea?"

"Remember the other day when you came in the dining room and I was watching News 12?"

"Noooooooooooooooooooo! Cornell? Cornell raped you?"

"Yes," I whispered.

"Damn – I went and told Jake and Rachel you cheated on me..."

"Well – Char thinks I cheated on you too..."

"You didn't tell her what happened?"

"I can't tell her."

"Why? She's your best friend."

"Yes she is – and her man raped me and I killed him..."

"All this time I thought you were worried about Char – my God Trenice – I can't believe you were actually comforting her over that bastard!"

"We can't tell her!"

"I won't tell her Trenice – but she's not stupid."

"I know – besides we have another problem."

"Now what?!" I pointed to the television as News 12 ran the story about the explosion again...

"Is that where it happened?"

I couldn't even answer him – I just burst into tears.

Jordan climbed into bed with me and held me while I cried. "Shhh... he can't hurt you anymore – he's dead."

"I know...I just hope he stay's dead."

"What do you mean Trenice?"

"It's only a matter of time before they discover one of those dead bodies is Cornell's."

"You killed him right there?"

"Hell yea – he didn't even see it coming."

"Well – you did everyone a favor..."

"I don't think Char will see it that way..."

"Oh my God – I forgot about that!"

"The worst part about this was not being able to tell you – I was so scared I infected you with HIV – then when I heard Sissy was pregnant all I could think about was me and Sissy giving birth at the same time and everyone commenting on how much the babies resembled each other..." I said as I started crying again...

"Shhh...I'm here Trenice – it's over now – it's all over..."

"I just hope they don't find out I killed him..."

"Trenice that explosion erased every bit of evidence you may have left there – I think you'll be ok..."

We sat in shock as they ran an update on News 12:

"We interrupt our regularly scheduled programming to bring you this update – this just in: Firefighters have determined that the cause of the explosion at the Getty Station on Mamaroneck Avenue in White Plains was due to arson. One of the bodies from the explosion has been identified as Cornell Jones. Cornell Jones has also been identified as the serial rapist here in Westchester. A photograph provided by his wife, Sissy Jones, matches the description and sketch provided by one of his victims. His DNA also matches the DNA found in the other victims. The Coroner's report states that although Cornell Jones' body was recovered from the explosion, he was killed by a blow to the head. The Coroner's report also states that, according to the decomposition of the body, Cornell Jones has been deceased for approximately 3 months. Stay tuned to News 12 for further updates. We now return to our regularly scheduled programming."

"Trenice?"

"Yes Jordan?" I said as I snuggled down underneath the covers with him.

"No more secrets."
"No more secrets. I promise."

Chapter 70

"Ahem!"

"Good morning nurse," I yawned.

"Honey, wake up," I said as I nudged Jordan.

"Morning," he yawned as he climbed out the bed.

"I need to check your vitals before the doctor gets here."

"What time will he be here?" I asked as she checked my blood pressure.

"Around 11," she said as she popped the thermometer in my mouth. When I beeped she took it out of my mouth, wrote some things in my chart, and left the room.

"Guess she didn't git none last night," Jordan laughed.

"And with that attitude she never will," I said as we both laughed.

"Now that's more like it," Char said as she came in and hugged us both.

"Good morning to you too Char," Jordan said.

"What time you gettin' outta here?"

"The doctor will be here 'round 11," I said.

"Everything ok right?"

"I think so. I gotta follow up with Dr. Campton and Dr. Campana though."

"Oh ok. They bring you breakfast yet?"

"No."

"Good," she said as she pulled out a McDonald's bag.

"Char that is so sweet – thank you!"

"You're welcome – hope you're hungry 'cause I got the breakfast deluxe," she laughed.

"Well if she's not – I am," Jordan laughed.

As we shared breakfast Char asked, "So when you get here Jordan?"

"I came last night."

"They let you stay?"

"Well after Trenice told the nurse I was her husband..."

"Aww...when I came in y'all looked so happy – I was surprised to see you."

"You think you were surprised? Shit – I didn't think I was ever gonna see him again," I laughed. Jordan opened the drawer to the nightstand to get some tissues. When he saw the song I wrote he picked it up, read it, and laughed to himself.

"What's so funny?" I asked. He reached into his coat pocket, pulled out a piece of paper, unfolded it, and gave it to me to read:

Too Late For Us

We can't go on fussing and fighting
We have to stop hurting and spiting.
We can't hold on to something not real.
I think we've lost what we feel.

Too Late For Us, Too Late For Us,
We just can't make it right.
Too Late For Us, Too Late For Us,
There's no love left in our lives....

I thought that love would last forever.
Breaking up no – oh no never.
But times have changed and so have we.
Where once dwelled love now dwells misery.

Ohhhh I'm sorry – sorry to say,
It had to end – end this way.
We can't go on living a lie,
The truth is that our love has died.

Too Late For Us, Too Late For Us,
We just can't make it right.
Too Late For Us, Too Late For Us,
There's no love left in our lives....

"Love letters?" Char asked.

"Somethin' like that," we both said in unison. Jordan put both songs in his pocket and we laughed at Jerry Springer and Maury until the doctor came in to release me.

"Good morning Trenice – you ready?"

"Hell yea!"

"These are our instructions – take Motrin for pain/fever and make sure you follow up with Dr. Campana."

"Ok."

"No heavy lifting, no strenuous activity, no tampons, no douching, and NO SEX FOR 6 WEEKS!"

"Yea right!" Char laughed.

"Your instructions are also written here – sign these and you're free to go...make sure your wife takes care of herself," he told Jordan.

"I'll do it so she doesn't have too," Jordan said as he pulled me into a kiss.

"NO SEX!" Char said as she laughed.

"Yea right!" we both said in unison.

When we got back home Jordan jumped in front of the door and unlocked it. When he picked me up I said, "Honey I'm ok – I can walk."

"And I can carry you," he said as he kicked the door open and carried me into the living room where he placed me on the sofa.

"Be careful Honey – you're gonna spoil me rotten..."

"I know," he laughed as he went into the kitchen.

"Trenice?"

"Yea?"

"What happened?"

"I can't talk about it now Char...I hope you understand..."

"Of course I understand – take all the time you need..." Just then, Jordan came into the living room with a pitcher of Kiwi Lemonade and 3 glasses.

"Thank you Char," he said as he sat down and poured the lemonade.

"For what?"

"For doing what I should have," he said as he hugged me.

"I'd do anything for Trenice – I love her."

"I love you too Char."

As we sipped our lemonade, Char asked, "Y'all see News 12?" I just sat there sipping my lemonade.

"Yea we saw it," Jordan said.

"So y'all know about Cornell?"

"Yea we know." Char sat there for a few minutes sipping her lemonade then she started again...

'Trenice?"

"Yea?"

"Why you ask me what company Cornell worked for?" I started choking on my lemonade and Jordan started slapping my back...

"You ok Trenice?" I coughed for a good 5 minutes before I said,

"Must'a went down the wrong windpipe."

"So why you ask me that Trenice?"

"I told you Char – I take taxis home all the time and figured maybe I saw him."

"You sure?"

"Char! Of course I'm sure!"

"I'm sorry..."

"That's ok."

"So did he ever take you home?"

"No Char." Well at least that wasn't a lie.

"I wonder who killed him…"

"Char, don't do this to yourself…"

"Trenice, you know damn well if it was Jordan you would wanna know…"

"You right Char, you right – I'm sorry…"

"No I'm sorry – you just got home from the hospital…"

"It's ok Char – I know how it feels when you need to get it out…"

"Whatchu need to get out Trenice?"

"Don't be tryin' to change the subject Char," I laughed.

"I think his wife did it."

"You do?" we both said in unison.

"Yea. I think she found about us and she hired someone…"

"Char you are crazy!" I laughed.

"Whatchu mean?"

"He was missing for a while right?"

"Yea?"

"He's found in a gas station that exploded due to arson?"

"Yea?"

"And there was another unidentified body recovered?"

Char sat for a minute and thought… "Oh my God – drugs!"

"I knew you'd figure it out," I lied. "Whew!" I said to myself. Just then, News 12 got our attention:

"We interrupt our regularly scheduled programming to bring you the following update: Friends and neighbors gathered at Cerrato Park on

Riverdale Avenue in Yonkers last night to light candles and say prayers for Cornell Jones. His wife, Sissy Jones, was too upset to comment; however, New 12 was notified that services will be held at Brooks Funeral Home on Warburton Avenue in Yonkers tomorrow from 4pm to 7pm. We now return to our regularly scheduled programming."

"I'm going," Char said.

"Do you think that's a good idea?" Jordan asked.

"I don't give a damn – I loved him and I need to say goodbye."

"Char what if Sissy makes a scene?"

"I'm not going there to cause trouble – I won't even stay long – I just wanna say goodbye."

"I'll go with you," I said.

"You will?" they both said in unison. Jordan looked at me like I lost my mind – which I must've to even offer to go – but it wasn't about Cornell – it was about Char.

"Yea Char – I'll go."

"I know how y'all felt about my relationship with him…"

"Look Char – you can't tell your heart what to do – shit happens," Jordan said.

"Besides – now we can all move on…"

"We?" Char asked. Shit! Why'd he have to go and say that?

"Yea – women can go back to feeling safe, Sissy can put closure on this, you can put closure on this, and Trenice can make you crazy."

"Watchu mean?"

"Char, you know damn well you throwin' her bridal shower," Jordan said as we all bust out laughing. Whew!

Chapter 71

"Trenice you sure about this?" Jordan asked as I was gettin' dressed.

"Not really."

"Why don't you tell Char you don't wanna go?"

"Cause I'm afraid of what will happen if I don't," I sighed.

"And I'm afraid of what will happen if you do," Jordan said as he pulled me into a hug. "I know you wanna be there for Char but are you gonna be able to sit there knowing that man raped you? And what about Sissy?"

"What about her?"

"How can you look at her?"

"I never really had a problem with Sissy – I just thought she was a nosy miserable bitch."

"Oh I see," Jordan laughed.

"She didn't have anything to do with her husband being a monster – it's more like the other way around – she's probably glad he's dead anyway."

"You think so?"

"I dunno," I sighed.

"I'm going with you."

"You are? You sure you can do this?"

"Only thing I'm sure of is I'll be glad when this shit is over."

"Me too."

"So you gonna tell Char what happened?"

"Not if I can help it…"

"She's gonna find out eventually – you know that right?'

"Yea I know," I said as we went out the door.

When we got to the funeral home we saw Sissy and Aunt Trudy first.

"Watchall doin' here?" Aunt Trudy asked.

"Hi Grandma, Hi Sissy," I said, ignoring her.

"Hi Trenice, Jordan – thanks for coming," Sissy said as she went to sit in the front.

"Hi Miss Gladys, Trudy," Jordan said as we turned to go outside. "I'll be glad when this shit is over," Jordan said.

"Me too," I said. Just then Char got out a cab and walked up to us.

"Hi guys," she said as Aunt Trudy, Grandma, and Sissy came outside with lit cigarettes.

"What the fuck you doin' here?" Sissy asked. We all turned to look at her in shock. "Don't play with me bitch – you think I don't know you was fuckin' my husband?"

"Get the fuck outta here!" Aunt Trudy said. "Trenice, why you bring her here if you knew what the fuck was goin' on? You don't have no fuckin' respect..."

"You don't have no fuckin' respect!' I yelled.

"Watch it Trenice," Grandma said.

"No I will not watch it either Grandma – first of all I didn't bring nobody here but myself – second of all I didn't know nothing about Sissy's husband until Aunt Trudy ran her fuckin' mouth tellin' Sissy's business – and she wanna say I have no fuckin' respect!"

"That's enough Trenice," Grandma said.

"No it isn't Grandma and you know it!" I yelled.

"Trenice shut the hell up now!" Aunt Trudy yelled.

"You shut the hell up – you the one that ran your mouth in the first place – I never asked you to tell me shit!"

"Trenice this is not the time or the place..."

"Well you didn't mind when Aunt Trudy was runnin' her mouth Grandma!"

"Trudy – what's goin' on here? What did you tell them?" Sissy asked.

"You little bitch!" Aunt Trudy yelled as she lunged for me...

"Trudy knock it off!" Grandma yelled as she put Aunt Trudy in a head lock..."

"Jordan let me go!" I yelled as he held me back.

"I'm tired of that bitch Ma – she always poppin' shit – let me go!" Aunt Trudy yelled.

"Maybe you should keep your fuckin' mouth shut instead of tryin' to tell me to shut the hell up!" I yelled back.

"Jordan take Trenice outta here – Trudy – get your ass inside – now!" Grandma yelled as she pushed Aunt Trudy through the door…

"Bitch you lucky Ma's here or I'd bust your ass!" she yelled when she got inside.

"I'll be waitin' when you come out bitch!" I yelled back.

"No you won't either Trenice – this is fuckin' ridiculous – I knew we should'a fuckin' stayed home!" Jordan said.

"I wish we did stay home – I don't fuckin' believe this shit!"

"Trenice?"

"What Sissy?"

"What did Trudy tell you?"

"She said your husband left you for another woman, he filed for a legal separation, and you might be pregnant."

"You lyin' bitch!"

"You think so? Ask Grandma – she was sittin' right there when Aunt Trudy told me – it was the same day I told y'all me and Jordan was gettin' married!"

"Didn't I tell you shut the fuck up bitch?" Aunt Trudy said as she charged into me, knocking me to the ground…

"Make me bitch!" I screamed as I kicked her in her stomach, knocking her back into one of the cars…

"I'll fuckin' kill you bitch!" she screamed as the lunged for me again…

We went fist for fist as we rolled around on the ground…

"Oh no you don't bitch!" my mother said as she snatched Aunt Trudy up off of me…

"Get the fuck off me Claire!" Aunt Trudy yelled as she punched my mother in the face.

"Oh I know you didn't hit my mother bitch!" I said as I lunged for her, knocking us all to the ground...

"Don't you ever put your hands on my daughter again!" my mother screamed as she punched Aunt Trudy in her face...

"Fuck you and your daughter!" she screamed as she punched my mother back in her face...

"What the hell is goin' on here? Claire, Trudy – break it up!" Grandma yelled... "Jordan – you lettin' them fight – why didn't you break it up?"

"For what? Trenice aiight – Claire aiight..."

"I said break it up dammit!" Grandma screamed as my mother and Aunt Trudy stood, glaring at each other. "Trenice you had no damn business..."

"Of course – it's all my fault – as usual!" I said sarcastically.

"No it isn't either – you had no business tellin' them my business Trudy!" Sissy yelled. "Miss Gladys you was right there too – you supposed to be my friend – don't blame this on Trenice – it's not her fault..."

"What's not her fault?" my mother asked.

"Never mind Claire," Grandma said...

"Aunt Trudy started this whole thing Ma..."

"Bitch shut the fuck up!" Aunt Trudy screamed...

"Anyway...she gonna say I have no respect 'cause I brought Char here – but she the one that told me and Grandma that Sissy's husband left her for another woman..."

"Oh so she runnin' her mouth but she wanna tell you shut the fuck up," my mother laughed.

"Exactly. So I'm telling Sissy what happened – next thing you know she charged me so we started fightin'..."

"I'll kick your ass again bitch!" Aunt Trudy yelled.

"You ain't kick it the first time bitch!" I yelled back.

"Jordan you didn't break it up?"

"Trenice was holdin' it down – she aiight," Jordan laughed.

"Claire get inside now!" Grandma yelled.

"I'll come when I'm ready Ma – why don't you go inside with Trudy?"

"Bitch I'm YOUR mother – you don't tell me..."

"Yea, yea yea – whatever Ma – go on inside," my mother laughed.

"Damn Ma – that's fucked up," I laughed.

"She'll get over it Trenice – you sure you alright?"

"Yea – I'm ok."

"So how long you been fuckin' my husband?" Sissy asked Char. We forgot all about Sissy and Char.

"About a year," Char answered.

"Oh I get it now," my mother said. "Trudy thinks you knew all along doesn't she?"

"Yea."

"You shouldn't have come here Char," Sissy said. "Trudy's right – you have no fuckin' respect..."

"I didn't come here to cause trouble. I didn't even know you were his wife until I saw your picture on News 12. I just came to say goodbye – if you want me to leave I will."

"Fuck it – you here now – you might as well stay," she laughed. "I actually feel kinda sorry for you."

"You should feel sorry for yourself – he told me he got a legal separation from you and he was filing for divorce so we could get married."

"And you believed him? Bitch please – you a bigger fool than I was," she laughed.

"Look – I know you upset but you got one more time to call me a bitch ok?"

"What the fuck you gonna do bitch?" she asked as she got up in Char's face. That was a bad move all the way around... "Huh bitch?"

"Char noooooooooo!" I yelled as she lunged for Sissy, grabbing by the throat, choking the shit out of her..."

"Gett the fuck off her bitch!" Aunt Trudy yelled as she grabbed Char from behind..."

"Get your fuckin' hands off me bitch!" she yelled as she lunged around, punching Aunt Trudy in the face. Next thing you know, they were rolling around going fist for fist on the ground. My mother and grandmother came running over to break it up...

"Ma let me go dammit!" Aunt Trudy yelled.

"Claire get off me!" Char yelled. "I'm aiight – lemme go!"

"Damn – was it that good? Was it worth all this?" Sissy asked. "Let me clear things up for you sweetie – he didn't get a legal separation from me – I got an order of protection on his ass – that's why he was stayin' with you."

"Fuck you!" Char yelled.

"No fuck you – 'cause that's about all he did for your ass!" Sissy laughed. "And as far as divorce papers? That's a crock of shit too – he got served with papers from family court 'cause he denied this baby I'm carrying," she laughed again. Just then, Tony walked up on us.

"Hi Trenice."

"Hi Tony. Did you know Cornell?"

"He was my brother," he said as he walked inside. Jordan and I just looked at each other without saying anything. Grandma and Aunt Trudy went inside with Sissy and my mother walked down Warburton Avenue with us.

"You ok Trenice?"

"Yea I'm ok Ma. I can't believe all this shit happened," I laughed. We all turned around when we heard Char crying.

"I can't believe I was so damn stupid," she cried.

"Char you didn't know," I said as I comforted her.

"I should'a left him when I found out he was married. Jordan tried to tell me but I didn't wanna believe it…"

"Char you not the first woman to make a fool out of herself over a man – and you certainly won't be the last," my mother said.

"Well it could'a been worse."

"How?" we all said in unison.

"I could'a been pregnant," she laughed.

"I can't believe all the shit that went down today," Jordan laughed.

"Me either," I laughed.

"Yea – the last thing I expected was to see you and Trudy rollin' around," my mother laughed.

"Trenice held her own though," Jordan laughed. "Ma dukes got a few licks in herself."

"I know Ma won't speak to any of us for a while," my mother laughed.

"Sorry Ma." I said.

"Shit – don't worry 'bout it Trenice – they'll get over it," she laughed again.

"I don't think so Ma. Grandma was real mad at me before you got here – now that you got in it she probably won't speak to you ever again."

"Trenice please – I'm a grown woman – I know that's my mother but you're my child and I'm gonna defend you regardless."

"I love you too Ma."

"Damn – I got all y'all in this shit – all 'cause I wanted somebody else's husband."

"Char we got along like this long before you started messin' with that man – it was gonna happen sooner or later," my mother said.

"I didn't go there to fight Aunt Trudy Ma – I really didn't – but when she came charging at me I didn't have a choice…"

"And I had no choice but to snatch her ass up off you," my mother laughed.

"I couldn't believe it when Char choked the shit outta Sissy," Jordan laughed.

"Yea – and Char and Trudy stared fightin' – damn!" my mother laughed.

"I'm sorry Miss Claire."

"Oh please Char – don't worry 'bout it – Sissy knew damn well her husband was sleeping around –

she'll have to get over that too," my mother laughed again.

"Miss Claire – you really don't give a damn do you?" Jordan asked.

"Hell no I don't give a damn – it's not like this is the first time we went somewhere and didn't know how to act," she laughed.

Chapter 72

We were laughing so hard we were holding our stomachs…

"Claire, you gotta be shittin' me!" Miss April said.

"No I'm not either April – I swear – the only one's that didn't fight was Jordan and Ma."

"I don't know why Gladys was expecting Jordan to break that shit up anyway – she know how Trudy is and she know how Trenice is – besides, Jordan wasn't gonna let Trudy or anybody else hurt Trenice," Miss June laughed.

"Damn right Mum!" Jordan said.

"What started all this anyway?" Miss April asked.

"All this started over Sissy's no good husband," my mother laughed.

"Figures – a no good man is always the cause of women fightin'," Miss April laughed. "So who did it this time?"

"Mum!" Jordan said.

"Well?" Miss April asked.

"Don't look at me," I laughed.

"Don't look at me either," my mother laughed.

"Well y'all gonna find out anyway so..."

Char started to tell them but she was interrupted by News 12:

"We interrupt our regularly scheduled program to bring you this update. As you can see, tempers flared earlier today as fights broke out earlier this evening at Cornell Jones' funeral. Cornell's wife, Sissy Jones, refused to comment on the cause of all the fighting, but News 12 has determined that Cornell's mistress showed up which we believe was the cause of all the fighting among friends and relatives. No arrests were made and no one plans on pressing charges. We now return to our regularly scheduled programming."

We all bust out laughing. "Claire did you see your hair?" Miss April laughed.

"Never mind my hair – did you see Trudy and Trenice goin' at it?"

"Damn – good thing Sissy ain't pressin' charges – they got my hands around her throat all up close 'n shit!" Char laughed.

"Well I guess we all know who the mistress is," Miss April laughed.

"Then damn – I guess I'm a celebrity now," Char laughed.

"Don't even worry about it Char – Sissy knew damn well he was no good when she met him," Miss June laughed,

"But God don't like ugly – that's why his ass is dead now," my mother laughed. We all got quiet. "What's wrong wichall?" my mother asked.

"Nothing – let's go see Jake and Rachel before we head home Honey," I said real quick.

"Ok – bye Mum-Mum – bye Miss Claire."

"Bye everybody," Char said.

"Char?"

"Yes Miss April?"

"The quickest way to get over a man..."

"Is to find another one!" we all yelled in unison. We all bust out laughing as we closed the door.

"You ok Char?" I asked.

"Yea I guess. I just can't believe I was so stupid!"

"Well at least you weren't stupid enough to get pregnant."

"Yea you right about that," she laughed. When we got to Char's house she said, "Y'all comin' up?"

"Naaa... we gotta stop at Jake and Rachels' – and we gotta get some rest," Jordan said.

"Alright – I'll call y'all tomorrow then – good night!"

"Good night Char!" we yelled in unison.

Jake and Rachel were sitting on the steps when we got there. "C'mon in Miss Ali," Rachel laughed.

"Oh you saw News 12?" Jordan laughed.

"We all saw News 12," Jake laughed.

"I can't believe this shit – this is like a fuckin' soap opera!" Jordan said.

"Well the best thing about all this is you two are back together," Jake said as he grabbed me up and gave me a hug."

"I didn't think I was ever gonna see Jordan again," I said.

"Well that's all behind us now," Jordan said.

"Trenice?"

"Yea Rachel?"

"What happened?"

"I can't talk about it Rachel...I just can't," I said as I started crying."

"Damn – sorry Trenice..."

"That's ok – it's not your fault..."

"Now I know something happened – you need me to fuck someone up for you?" Jake asked.

"No that's ok – I'll be alright – Jordan will make sure of that – right honey?"

"Right," he said as he pulled me into a kiss.

"You sure y'all alright?"

"Yea – we'll be fine," Jordan said.

"Tell 'em." I said.

"You sure?"

"Yea... I guess. Besides – my secret's safe with them – isn't it?" I asked as I looked Jake and Rachel directly in the eyes...

"Damn Trenice – you're scaring me..." Rachel said.

"You haven't been scared yet," I whispered.

"Who hurt you Trenice?" Jake yelled. "I'll fuckin' kill him!"

"I already did."

"Huh?" Jake and Rachel said in shock.

"He raped me – so I killed him."

"Who?" Jake asked.

"Cornell," Jordan answered.

"Muthafucka!" Jake yelled. "You never reported it?"

"No."

"Damn – and I thought you cheated on Jordan..."

"So does Char..."

"You didn't tell her?"

"I can't."

"Why Trenice? She's your best friend," Rachel said.

"And that was her man," I said.

"Oh my God... you mean..."

"Yea."

"She hasn't asked you what happened?"

"Yea."

"What you say?"

"I said I can't talk about it."

"She's smart – she's gonna put 2 and 2 together eventually."

"I'll deal with eventually when it gets here."

"I'm surprised you haven't had a nervous breakdown Trenice – I couldn't imagine keeping that all bottled up inside."

"I'm just glad you told Jordan to go see Dr. Campton." I said.

"You are?" they both said in unison.

"Yea – that's what got Jordan to the hospital in the first place," I said as I leaned into Jordan.

"All this shit went down – everybody fightin' n shit – and Cornell is at the center of it all," Jake said.

"You remember Tony?" Jordan asked.

"Tony... no I don't think I know him..." Jake said.

"Isn't that the guy you were talkin' too before you and Jordan got together Trenice?" Rachel asked.

"Yea."

"Why – you need me to fuck him up for you Trenice?" Jake laughed.

"Cornell was Tony's brother," Jordan said.

"Damn Trenice – I see why you can't tell anybody," Jake said.

"Well at least your mother was there for you when the shit went down. I wonder how your grandmother would feel if she found out Cornell raped you – I bet she wouldn't be defending Trudy then," Rachel said.

"She'll never find out – 'cause I'll never tell her!"

"I'm sorry Trenice."

"No I'm sorry – I'm glad this is all over and we can get back to our lives."

"Amen!" Jordan said.

"Trenice?"

"Yea Rachel?"

"How did you…"

"The less you know the better."

"Fair enough."

"Well we better go," Jordan said as we got up.

"Alright – take care – call us if you need us," Jake said as we all hugged each other.

Chapter 73

"Hi Honey," I said as I closed the door behind me.

"Hey Beautiful," Jordan said as he pulled me close to him and kissed me.

"Mmmmm….. This is nice," I said as I started kissing his neck…

"Come sit down Trenice," Jordan said as he took me into the living room.

"Shaliyah! This is a pleasant surprise," I said as I opened my arms. When she ran to me and threw her arms around me, bursting into tears, I got really scared. "How long has she been here?" I whispered.

"About an hour."

"Did she say anything?"

"She just said she needs to talk to you Trenice."

"So she's just been sitting here?"

"Yea. I turned on the Disney Channel but she wasn't really watching it."

"It'll be okay Shaliyah – we'll take care of it," I said as I stroked her hair and she continued to cry. "You want something to drink Shaliyah?"

"Uh uh," she said between sobs.

"Is Mommy okay Shaliyah?"

"Uh huh," she said as she continued to cry.

"Shaliyah?"

"Huh?"

"Are you ok?"

"Nooooooooooooooooo…" she said as she started crying even harder.

"Jordan?"

"Yea?"

"Is that what I think it is?"

"What Trenice?"

"Right there!" I said as I pointed to the blood stains on the floor.

"Oh my God – its blood – Shaliyah – why didn't you tell me you were hurt – we gotta get you to the hospital – who did it? – I'll fuckin' kill 'em – Trenice, call your mother and have her meet us at the hospital – Shaliyah you come with me and…"

"Jordan – stop it!"

"Trenice – we have to get her to the hospital…"

"No we don't…"

"Why not? Can't you see she's bleeding for God's sake?"

"She has her period."

"Her period?"

"I got my period?" Shaliyah asked through tear-soaked eyes.

"Yes Shaliyah – you have your period. Did Mommy talk to you about your period yet?"

"I'll clean this up while you two talk," Jordan laughed. "I was ready to rush her to the hospital and go kill someone," he laughed again and shook his head as he walked out the living room into the kitchen.

"Mommy told me about my period but I didn't know I was gonna bleed Trenice," Shaliyah said.

"I thought you said Mommy explained it to you Shaliyah," I said as I led her to the bathroom.

"She did Trenice – but she didn't tell me I was gonna bleed – she just said I would have to wear the special pads and I gotta make sure I change 'em."

"Here Shaliyah – take off your skirt and panties – take this and wash yourself up," I said as I took a box of Always pads out of the bathroom closet and set it on the toilet. "Do you know how to put the pad on?"

"Uh huh – Mommy showed me," she said as she pulled one of the pads out of the box, pulled the strip off the pad, put it in her clean panties, and pulled them up.

"Everything ok in there Shaliyah?" Jordan yelled.

"I'm ok!" Shaliyah yelled back as she finished gettin' dressed. "Trenice?"

"Yes Shaliyah?"

"What do I do with these?"

"You have to wash them out in cold water with soap."

"Can I do it when I get home?"

"No Shaliyah – you have to do it right away – otherwise the blood won't come out."

"What if it happens when I'm in school?"

"If you have an accident in school you go to the nurse and the nurse will call Mommy so you can go home and you don't have to walk around with blood on your clothes."

"Trenice?"

"Yes Shaliyah?"

"How do I know when to change the pad?"

"You change it when it gets full of blood."

"Trenice?"

"Yes Shaliyah?"

"What if it gets full of blood and I'm in school? How will I be able to change it?"

"When you get your period you carry some pads in your book bag or ask Mommy for a little pocketbook."

"Trenice?"

"Yes Shaliyah," I answered as I took her by the hand and we went back to the living room.

"What if I forget the pads?"

"You go to the nurses' office and she will give you some."

"Thank you Trenice," she said as she hugged me.

"You're welcome," I said as I hugged her back.

"I was soooo scared," she said.

"I bet – if you don't know what to expect it can be a scary thing," Jordan said.

"Trenice?"

"Yes Shaliyah?"

"My stomach hurts."

"That's because you have cramps."

"What's a cramp?"

"You know that feeling you get when you have diarrhea?"

"Uh Huh!"

"Cramps are like that."

"Do you get cramps Trenice?"

"Every woman gets cramps Shaliyah."

"I'm a woman?" she asked with beaming eyes.

"Shaliyah you're only 10 years old – you won't be a woman until you're 21."

"Shoot!" she said with a frown as we laughed.

"Don't rush it Shaliyah – enjoy being a kid while you can," Jordan laughed.

"Oh I will now that I know I'm not pregnant."

"Pregnant!" we both yelled in unison.

"Whatever made you think you were pregnant Shaliyah?" I asked.

"Mommy said I better stay away from boys."

"Well Shaliyah she's right." I said.

"No she isn't Trenice."

"Shaliyah you're way too young to be foollin' around with boys..."

"I don't fool around with boys!" she yelled.

"Ok Shaliyah – I'm sorry – I'm not accusing you of anything – but you said..."

"I told Mommy there's a new boy in my class and his name is Richard."

"Well that's nice," I said.

"I told Mommy Richard sat next to me at lunch time and we were playing on the school ground at recess."

"Nothing wrong there," Jordan said.

"I didn't think so either – but Mommy said I better stay away from boys and play with girls."

"Oh so you thought you were pregnant because you played with Richard at school?"

"No Trenice! Listen!"

"Ok Shaliyah – I'm sorry – go 'head."

"Mommy said you start out playin' with boys – next thing you know you're kissin' boys – next think you know you're pregnant!"

"Shaliyah?"

"Yes?"

"Did you kiss Richard?" I asked. She didn't answer right away. She bit her bottom lip and looked down.

"I didn't know he was gonna do that," she said.

"Do what Shaliyah? What did Richard do?"

"He kissed me right here," she said as she pointed to her right cheek. "He said I was nice. Are you gonna tell Mommy?" she asked with tears in her eyes.

"No Shaliyah – I won't tell Mommy – but no more kissin' boys – understand?"

"Understand!" she yelled.

"Trenice?"

"Yes Shaliyah?"

"How do you get pregnant?"

"Oh boy – here it comes," Jordan said as he shook his head."

"Something's coming?" Shaliyah asked.

"No, no, no Shaliyah – nothing's coming," I laughed.

"What's so funny Trenice?"

"Nothing Shaliyah."

"Then why did you laugh?" she asked.

"Cause Jordan's funny."

"Trenice?"

"Yes Shaliyah?"

"How do you get pregnant?"

"Shaliyah do you know what a penis is?"

"Uh huh."

"Do you know what a vagina is?"

"Uh huh."

"Well if a boy puts his penis in your vagina then you get pregnant."

"I thought boys only use their penis to go to the bathroom," Shaliyah laughed. "Trenice?"

"Yes Shaliyah?"

"Why do we get periods?"

"That's a little hard to explain Shaliyah – you'll find our more about that when you're a little older."

"But I wanna know now," she whined.

"Well, since we are the ones that have to carry the babies, our bodies have to get ready."

"Oh so I'm gettin' ready to have a baby?"

"Kinda."

"But I'm not pregnant right?"

"No Shaliyah – you're definitely not pregnant."

"I can only get pregnant if a boy puts his penis in my vagina right?"

"Right."

"Trenice?"

"Yes Shaliyah?"

"The boy puts his penis in your vagina to make you pregnant right?"

"Yes."

"So how does the baby get there?"

"That's a little hard to explain Shaliyah ..."

"I'll find out when I get older right?"

"Yes! Exactly!" I said as I breathed a sigh of relief.

"Trenice?"

"Yes Shaliyah?"

"Why did Mommy say you start out playin' with boys – next thing you know you're kissn' boys – next thing you know – you're pregnant?"

"Because if you kiss a boy a lot he's gonna think it's ok to put his penis in your vagina."

"Oh ok… I don't want Richard to do that – I won't play with him anymore!" she yelled.

"Shaliyah you can play with Richard and the other kids in your class – just don't kiss the boys that's all," Jordan said.

"What if they wanna kiss me?"

"You tell them you said no!" Jordan said.

"What if they do it anyway?"

"Then you tell them if they do it again you're gonna tell the teacher and you won't be their friend anymore."

"Ok!" she yelled.

"Trenice?"

"Yes Shaliyah?"

"You and Jordan always kiss," she laughed.

"Yes we do," I said.

"Does Jordan want to put his penis in your vagina?"

"Pffffffffffffttttttttt… cough…cough…cough…"

"Honey are you ok?" I laughed.

"Yea – I just choked on my juice," Jordan laughed.

"No Shaliyah – Jordan doesn't want to put his penis in my vagina."

"Why not? Don't you wanna have a baby?"

"Maybe one day," I said as Jordan and I looked at each other. We all jumped when the phone rang…

"Hello?"

"Trenice? Is Shaliyah over there?"

"Hi Ma – yea, she's here…"

"I'ma beat her ass when she gets home – she knows she's not supposed to…"

"Ma she got her period," I interrupted.

"She did? When?"

"Earlier this afternoon – Jordan picked her up from school."

"How's she doin'?"

"She's ok Ma – she changed her clothes and put a pad on."

"Poor thing – le'me talk to her…"

"Here Shaliyah – Mommy wants to talk to you," I said as I gave her the phone…

"Hi Mommy… Uh huh… Uh huh… okay Mommy – bye."

"Ready to go home Shaliyah?" I asked.

"Yea."

"Okay – Honey I'm gonna take her home then I'll be right back ok?"

"Okay Beautiful," he said as he kissed me then kissed Shaliyah on the cheek.

"No!" she yelled.

"I'm sorry Shaliyah," Jordan said as he backed away from her.

"I'm just kidding!" she laughed as she gave him a hug.

Chapter 74

The phone startled me as usual. I waited until the room stopped spinning and for the pounding in my head to subside as I waited for the answering machine to come on. After the phone rang for the 12th time, I had no choice but to get up and answer it – otherwise I would have had a migraine headache along with my coffee.

"Hello?' I yawned into the phone.

"Hey girl – what's up?"

"Oh hi Char."

"You up for company?"

"Not really."

"Oh."

"Girl you know you can come over here anytime you want too," I laughed.

"But you said you're not up for company."

"I know but that doesn't mean – girl git your ass over here," I laughed before I hung up the phone.

When Char got there she could smell the coffee right away. "Mmm... that smells good – what is it?"

"Hazelnut."

"You got half & half?"

"I got that and Amaretto – which do you prefer?"

"I prefer to stay sober 'till at least 12 noon," she laughed as she followed me into the kitchen. I made 2 cups of coffee, passed one to Char, and we went into the dining room and sat at the table.

"Nothing like fresh brewed coffee to wake up the senses and alleviate stress," I said as I sipped my coffee.

"I'm surprised we don't smoke too," Char said as she sipped her coffee.

"I never did like cigarettes Char."

"Me either Trenice."

"When I was little my Grandma used to always tell me – here – go light this cigarette for me," I laughed.

"I think all grandmothers do that," she laughed.

"Yea – but her cigarette would always go out and she'd tell me I have to pull on it a little bit to keep it lit," I laughed.

"Then Damn! I'm surprised you didn't start sneakin' a cigarette for yourself and smokin' it later," she laughed.

"I never even thought about it Char – but when I made her coffee and started tastin' it I was hooked!" I laughed.

"I hear that – I started drinkin' coffee when I was 12!"

"Me too!" We laughed for a few minutes then Char said, "Well at least we don't have to worry about lung cancer."

"Not at all – we just have to worry about excess weight, irritable bowel syndrome, ulcers, dehydration, and heart palpitations," I laughed.

"Then damn – how you know all that shit?"

"I read it at the doctor's office – caffeine does all that stuff."

"How does it make you gain weight?"

"It doesn't make you gain weight – it messes with your metabolism so you have problems losing weight."

"What about dehydration? How you dehydrated if you drinkin'?"

"The caffeine depletes your bodily fluids quickly – unless you're in the habit of drinkin 8 to 10 glasses of water a day."

"Then damn – maybe we should switch to decaffeinated..."

"Naaa....," we both said in unison.

We both sat at the table and finished the pot of coffee while we watched Jerry Springer and Maury.

"I can't believe those people wanna tell all the world their business," Char laughed.

"Well if they wanna tell it I wanna hear it," I laughed.

"I know one thing – my daughter wouldn't be goin' on no damn TV talking 'bout she slept with over 20 guys and she don't know who her baby daddy is."

"I hear that – bad enough the town know she a hoe – now 600 million people know she a hoe!" I laughed.

"Then they wanna cry and scream – I know they all watch the show – they know the guys gonna call 'em hoes!"

"What gets me is when the momma's come on the show talking 'bout my son this and my son that – they need to be tellin' their son's use a damn condom!"

"Ya know? My momma always told me – if you gonna be a hoe – be a good hoe – use condoms – then you don't show up in the doctor's office or family court and everyone ain't got to know your damn business!" Char laughed. Then she got real quiet.

"Char? What's wrong? Char?"

"I don't believe this fuckin' shit!"

"What Char? Whaatttt!!!"

"I never got pregnant Trenice!"

"And that's a bad thing?"

"No it's not – but he told me he wanted children..."

"I thought you were glad you didn't get pregnant?"

"I am!"

"Then why are you so mad?"

"Cause if I was tryin' to get pregnant and we didn't use nothin' – how the fuck is Sissy pregnant?" I thought about it for a minute...

"Then damn!"

"Now you got it?"

"Ain't this a bitch – the pot callin' the mothafuckin' kettle black!"

"That's what I'm talkin about!"

"Everybody feelin' sorry for Sissy n shit – even me – and she ain't no better than Cornell!" I laughed.

"Well she 'bout to cash in 'cause she got his name and she got pregnant before he died so she'll get survivor benefits for that child along with the other ones."

"I told Jordan she was probably glad he was dead!"

"You did? When did you say that?"

"Before we went to his funeral."

"Oh."

"You really wanted his baby?"

"Yea."

"Damn Char."

"Please don't start Trenice."

"I'm not...but..."

"But what?"

"Well..."

"What Trenice? Just say it dammit!"

"Ok – but remember I love you ok?"

"Of course...now what the hell you wanna know?"

"Have you been tested?"

"I know I'm not pregnant Trenice..."

"That's not what I mean..."

"Yea – I was tested a couple months ago.

"But that was before Char."

"Yea? So?"

"So what if he gave you something Char? You need to get tested again."

"Trenice?"

"Yea?"

"Why did you get tested again?" Shit! I knew she was gonna start on that...

"Don't be tryin' to change the subject missy," I laughed.

"Stop it Trenice."

"Stop what Char?"

"Stop lyin' to me!"

"Char why in the world would I lie to you?"

"You tell me..."

"Tell you what Char? What have I lied to you about?"

"You right Trenice – I shouldn't accuse you of lying."

"Exactly."

"But I know damn well you not telling me everything either."

"Char, you're my best friend."

"I know but..."

"But nothing! You are the only person I confide in and you've never betrayed me..."

"Yes but..."

"There you go buttin' me again! I know we've been friends for a long time and I also know I don't know every intimate detail of your life – and you know what Char?"

"What Trenice?"

"I don't care!"

"Watchumean you don't care?" she asked as she started crying...

"Oh my God Char – what is wrong with you! I never said I don't care about you – I just said I don't care if you don't tell me every little intimate detail of your life!"

"Why?"

"Because some things should stay between you and God, Char."

"Trenice I don't get you…"

"Char!"

"What?"

"How many men have you slept with?"

"That's none of your fuckin' business!"

"Exactly!"

"Huh?"

"Just because were best friends doesn't mean I feel like you're keeping something from me 'cause you won't tell me how many men you've slept with – only you and God know – understand?"

"I guess…but if you really wanna know…"

"No Char – I don't wanna know – ugh!" I said as I threw up my hands in frustration.

"What's wrong with you?"

"Nothing! And there's nothing wrong with you either!"

"Trenice I know what you're up to…"

"Ok detective – what am I up to?"

"You tryin' not to answer my question."

"And what question is that Char?"

"I answered yours…"

"Yes you did – you told me it was none of my fuckin' business!" I laughed.

"So is that how you feel?"

"Watchu mean?" I asked mocking her.

"Do you feel like it's none of my fuckin' business why you got tested again?"

"No Char."

"So answer the question then."

"Why?"

"Why what?"

"Why do you need to know so bad Char? What's bothering you?"

"I don't know...nothing...everything...I don't know!"

"Char?"

"Yea?"

"I got tested again because it was necessary."

"Oh."

"Trenice?"

"Yea?"

"You said you should've told Jordan before..."

"Yea."

"Then you said - how could I do this to him..."

"Yea."

"Then you said you were confused..."

"Yea."

"Then you said you didn't cheat on Jordan..."

"Yea."

We sat in silence for a few minutes.

"I gotta go Trenice – I'll see you later."

"Ok Char," I said to her back as she closed the door behind her.

Chapter 75

I don't remember what time I went to sleep but when I woke up and looked around it was dark and someone was pounding on the door... "Use your key!" I yelled as I lay back down...

"We don't have one!"

"Shaliyah? Is that you?" I said as I jumped up and ran to the door...

"Surprise!" My mother, brothers and sisters, Miss April, Miss June, Jake, and Rachel were all standing in the doorway...

"Trenice?"

"Yes Ma?"

"You gonna invite us in or you gonna leave us in the hallway?"

"Ohhh...sorry," I laughed, "C'mon in."

"We wake you up Trenice?"

"Yea – but that's ok – it's time for me to get up anyway – Jordan will be home soon." Just as I said that we heard Jordan's key in the door...

"Hey everybody! Hey Beautiful!" he said as he kissed me. "How long y'all been here?"

"We just got here," Miss April said. "So what's for dinner Jordan?" my mother asked.

"We can come up with something Miss Claire – right Trenice?"

"Sure we can."

"Well hurry up and make up your mind so we can call and have it delivered – you know you call them after a certain hour and instead of 10-20 minutes you gotta wait 45 minutes to an hour," my mother said.

"True, True," I laughed.

"Can we have pizza Mommy?"

"It's their treat Shaliyah – they get to pick."

"Oh that's nice – thank you Miss Claire," Jordan said.

"You're welcome – now hurry up!" she laughed.

"What else do you like besides pizza Shaliyah?" Jordan asked.

"Well...I like cheeseburgers, French fries, and Chinese food!"

"Well then – how 'bout McDonalds?"

"Oh yea!"

"Alrighty but they don't deliver – so y'all tell me whatchu want so we can go git it," my mother said.

"We?" Miss April asked.

"Now Ma you know damn well me 'n Claire gonna git the food and you gonna git the liquor," Miss June laughed.

"You got cards Trenice?" Miss April asked.

"Yep."

"Can you play spades?"

"It's gonna be a long, long night..." Jordan laughed as my mother, Miss April, and Miss June went out the door...

"So how youse been?" Jake asked.

"We're ok."

"What's wrong Trenice?"

"Nothing really."

"Oh boy – I don't like the sound of this," Jordan said.

"What happened now?" Rachel asked. I looked around to make sure my brothers and sisters were in the living room watching TV. My oldest brother, Marlowe, was blasting the stereo.

"Marlowe, I can't hear the cartoon," Shaliyah whined.

"Sit closer to the TV then," he said. I knew they would be alright so I motioned for them to come into the dining room. When we sat down at the table I started to explain...

"Char was here earlier."

"How's she doin'?" Jordan asked.

"I'm not sure."

"Oh boy..."

"I tried to avoid it but she wouldn't let up so I just told her."

"You told her Cornell raped you?" Rachel asked.

"Not exactly."

"Well what exactly did you say Trenice?" Jordan asked.

"I said I got tested again because it was necessary."

"What she say?"

"She just started askin' me questions about that night."

"What night?"

"When she took me to the hospital."

"Oh – that night."

"Yea."

"So what you say?"

"I just said 'yea' every time she asked me a question."

"I knew it was a matter of time," Rachel said.

"Well after I said 'yea' about 6 times, she got up and left."

"So you really think she knows?"

"Yea – she knows – the only question she didn't ask me was if Cornell raped me."

"Thank God." Jordan said. Just then Shaliyah came running into the kitchen...

"Trenice?"

"Yes Shaliyah?"

"Can I watch the Disney Channel?"

"Sure you can."

"Ok...Marlowe – Trenice said I can watch the Disney Channel!"

"No you can't either!"

"I'll be back," I said as I went into the living room...

"Trenice, I'm not letting her watch the Disney Channel – I don't care what you say!"

"Fine with me – but you know when Ma comes in here..."

"Here Shaliyah go 'head!" he said as he threw the remote.

"Don't throw my shit Marlowe."

"Ohhhh...you said a bad word..." Shaliyah said.

"Shut up!" we both yelled in unison. We laughed as Shaliyah quietly sat down with the remote and turned to the Disney Channel. Just then my mother and Miss June came in with the food and Miss April came in behind them with a few bottles of Bacardi and a few bottles of Pepsi. We ate until every last bit of the food was gone.

"Alright – y'all git in the living room so we can get our game on," Miss April laughed.

"Shaliyah?"

"Yes Trenice?"

"You can go watch TV in my room but you have to promise you won't touch anything ok?"

"I promise!" she yelled as she skipped down the hall.

"Jake/Rachel vs Mum/Mum." Jordan said. "Trenice/Miss Claire play the winners."

"I can't believe you still call them Mum-Mum," Jake laughed as they all sat down. We all laughed as Jake and Rachel whipped them to shame.

"Aiight Ma – let's do this," I said as we sat down.

"Do what Trenice? Cry when you lose?" Rachel laughed.

"Kick they ass Claire!" Miss April yelled.

When we whipped them back Jordan said, "Jake/Rachel vs Trenice/Miss Claire – final match. Winner of this game is tonight's champion.

"Don't try that shit again Trenice," Rachel laughed.

"Whatsa matter Rachel? Can't stand a little competition?" my mother laughed.

"We'll see how you stand after we whip dat ass!" Rachel laughed. Unfortunately for them, it was no contest.

"The winner and champion for tonight is Trenice/Miss Claire!"

"You won Trenice? Ohhh yea!" Shaliyah yelled as she came running into the kitchen, hugging us both.

"Oh shut up," Rachel laughed.

"Rachel you know damn well Trenice is a tourney champion in the gaming zone – and who do you think taught her what she knows?"

"I know that's right Ma," I laughed as we slapped each other high 5's.

"Aiight – you got that," Jake said as he shook our hands.

"Damn right we did," I laughed.

"Try that shit again next week," Rachel laughed.

"Aiight y'all – lets get goin' – it's gettin' late," my Mother yawned. We all exchanged hugs and kisses at the door as everyone said goodbye.

When they all left, I followed Jordan into the dining room and just sat there quiet as he cleaned up everything. When he was finished he come over to me, took me by the hand, and led me into the bedroom. Jordan was kinda surprised at how quickly I undressed and got into bed. Naturally, he undressed and climbed into bed with me just as quickly.

"Come here my Spades Queen," he said as he pulled me close to him, kissing me as he did so. "What's wrong Trenice?"

"Nothing really."

"Trenice you made me a promise," he said as he sat up.

"And I intend to keep it," I said as I sat up next to him.

"So why do I feel like you're not telling me something?"

"I dunno," I said as I snuggled up under him and he wrapped his arm around me. "Char was tryin' to get pregnant."

"Trenice?"

"Yea?"

"Let's not talk about Char tonight," he said.

"We have too."

"Oh boy – I knew there was something," he signed. "So when did she tell you this?"

"Today."

"Ok – so what's the problem?"

"Well, if she's been tryin' to get pregnant all this time..."

"How could she be so stupid?"

"Jordan let me..."

"No Trenice! I swear she gets on my fuckin' nerves..."

"Jordan?"

"What Trenice?"

"I made you a promise right?"

"Yes Trenice," he sighed.

"Okay then – now where was I?"

"She was tryin' to get pregnant..."

"Yea – but she didn't."

"So why do you care Trenice?"

"Well, Char says if she didn't get pregnant and they were tryin' all this time..."

"Yea?"

"Then how did Sissy get pregnant?"

"Trenice?"

"Yea?"

"What does this have to do with us?"

"You don't get it do you?"

"Get what Trenice?"

"If Cornell didn't get Char pregnant then he didn't get Sissy pregnant."

"So what?"

"So then he didn't get me pregnant either," I said with tears in my eyes. "I lost our baby Jordan...I lost our baby!" I said again as we both cried.

Chapter 76

The next morning was unusually quiet. Jordan noticed my mood right away.

"You ok Trenice?"

"Yea... I guess..."

"We'll be alright Beautiful," he said as he pulled me into a hug.

"I love you too," I said as we hugged each other.

"You want some breakfast?"

"Sure."

"Ok – I'll go make us some."

"Jordan?"

"Yea?"

"You ok?"

Jordan went into the kitchen without answering me. I got up and went into the dining room and sat down to use the phone. When Jordan came back into the dining room, he heard the end of the conversation... "You can see me today at 3 p.m.? Okay – we'll be there."

"Who was that Trenice?"

"That was Dr. Campana's office."

"Dr. Campana? Isn't that your gynecologist?"

"Yea."

"You sure you wanna see her so soon Trenice?"

"Not really."

"So what made you call her then?"

"I'm gettin' a headache..."

"Ok – let's eat."

"Ok."

"3 p.m. huh?"

"Yea."

"Well it's 12:30 now – we'll make it on time."

We finished breakfast and got dressed without saying a word. We didn't even speak to each other when we got in the car and drove to the doctor's office. When we got there, the receptionist started in with the questions...

"So what brings you here today Trenice?"

"I'd rather wait to speak with the doctor."

"She's gonna ask me why you're here and I need to tell her something..."

"I'll wait for the doctor."

"What is it Trenice? A yeast infection? An STD? You think you're pregnant?" Oh boy. She should've never said that...

"Bitch what the fuck is your problem?"

"Excuse me?"

"Didn't she say she'll wait for the doctor?"

"I'm just doing my job..."

"No you're just being fuckin' nosy…" Just then Dr. Campana came out into the waiting area…

"Sir, if you don't calm down I'll have to ask you to leave…"

"Honey calm down – it's okay…"

"Trenice is he with you?"

"Yes."

"Well he can't abuse my staff…"

"Well the bitch need to mind her business then…"

"Jordan stop it!"

"Trenice come into my office…"

"Ok."

When I got up and Jordan started to follow me Dr. Campana said, "You wait here."

"Like hell I will!"

"Jordan calm down!" I said.

"I can see you're upset but I won't tolerate you abusing my staff – is that understood?"

"Whatever."

"Trenice what's going on here?"

"We'll talk inside Dr. Campana."

"Ok – but if he's coming with you he has to behave himself."

"Whatever."

"C'mon Jordan – let's get this over with," I said as we went into her office.

"Dr. Campana this is my husband, Jordan."

"Husband? Congratulations! When did you get married?"

"We haven't set a date yet."

"Well what brings you here today? You're not due for another PAP for a few months – are you pregnant?" I burst into tears.

"Don't cry Trenice," Jordan said as he comforted me.

"Did I say something to upset you Trenice? What's going on?"

"I don't know where to start Dr. Campana."

"Just start at the beginning Trenice."

"Ok. You remember the last time we were here?"

"Vaguely."

"Remember you told me you wish more of your patients were like us?"

"You two had sex in the bathroom!"

"We never had sex in the bathroom Dr. Campana."

"Yea right Trenice," she laughed.

"Didn't she just tell you we never had sex in the bathroom? Damn!"

"Oh boy – your husband's gettin' upset again – this must be serious – I'm sorry – go ahead Trenice."

"Well our test came back negative so we were good to go."

"Ok."

"So when I went to the emergency room a few months back I thought I had the flu but I found out I was pregnant."

"Was?"

"Let her finish please Dr."

"Ok – I'm sorry – go ahead Trenice."

"Well I was happy until I found out I was 2 months pregnant."

"I don't understand Trenice."

"Well if I was only 1 month pregnant I would've been happy but once the Dr. told me I was 2 months pregnant, that's when I knew…"

"What Trenice?"

"I knew it was possible that Jordan wasn't the father of my baby," I said as I started crying again...

"Oh Trenice – I'm sorry...I had no idea...

"And you won't have any idea if you keep interrupting her Dr..."

"Why are you being so hostile? I'm on your side, remember?"

"I'm sorry Dr. – go 'head Trenice – tell her."

"I was raped about the same time I got pregnant Dr. Campana."

"Oh my God! Trenice I'm sorry!"

"Dr. Campton tested me again for HIV and the test came back negative but he said Jordan and I needed to be tested again in 3 months."

"Have you been tested yet?"

"No – it hasn't been 3 months yet."

"Ok."

"So I asked the doctor to call me to remind me to come in but that fuckin' receptionist sent a letter to my house!"

"What's wrong with that Trenice?"

"Jordan found the letter."

"Oh I see."

"So we ended up having a bad fight and I had to be carried to St. John's hospital in an ambulance."

"Oh my God!"

"I lost the baby Dr. Campana," I said as I started crying again.

"Trenice, Im so sorry. Now I understand why your husband is so upset."

"No you don't either," Jordan said.

"Jordan I'm trying too..."

"You wanna know why I'm upset? I'll tell you why I'm upset!"

"Ok, ok..."

"Trenice tells her she wants to wait until she sees you. She says you gonna ask her so Trenice needs to tell her something. Trenice says she wants to wait for you so she gonna ask her in front of everyone if she got a yeast infection, if she got an STD, or if she pregnant!"

"What?"

"Yea – she askin' Trenice that in front of everybody so that's when I asked her what the fuck her problem was!"

"No wonder your husband's upset – I'll deal with her later today – you have every right to be upset – how dare she?"

"Dr. Campana its ok..."

"No it isn't Trenice – and I can guarantee you I'll take care of it – it won't happen again!"

"Dr. Campana?"

"Yes Trenice?"

"Can I finish now?"

"I'm sorry Trenice – go ahead."

"When I had the miscarriage they said I may have some blockage – they told me I could wind up with an infection and my chances of gettin' pregnant again would be slim to none," I said as I started crying again.

"They told me the same thing Trenice..."

"Huh?" we both said in unison.

"A few years ago I had a miscarriage and I wound up with an infection. They couldn't save my fallopian tube so I had to have it taken out along with the ovary."

"Wow – I'm sorry Dr. Campana. Are you ok?"

Dr. Campana got up from behind the desk and said, "I'll see you in the examination room."

We waited for a few minutes until Dr. Campana returned. Jordan held my hand and we looked into each other's eyes as Dr. Campana examined me. She didn't have to ask if she was hurting me 'cause when she pushed down on my right side, I yelled so loud the lab techs and nurses came bursting into the room...

"Is she ok Dr. Campana?"

"She needs an ultra sound right away."

"Ok Dr." Jordan never let go of my hand.

"Nurse?"

"Yes Dr.?"

"Send this over to the lab."

"Ok Dr."

"Trenice we're almost finished –hang in there..."

"I don't have a choice do I?" I mumbled.

"Ok Trenice – you can get dressed now," she said as she left the room. When we went back to her office she had the pictures up for us to look at. "Everything looks okay, but you do have some swelling here," she said as she pointed to one of the pictures. "What did they say at the hospital?"

"They said I needed a D & C."

"Oh ok – that explains it then."

"Explains what Dr.?" Jordan asked.

"They did a D & C to remove any excess tissue so she wouldn't get an infection – this is a normal picture of a uterus, fallopian tubes, and ovaries – now look at Trenice's pictures..."

"Ok."

"See this area here?"

"Yea."

"The swelling will go down in a few weeks. Did they give you any antibiotics Trenice?"

"Yea."

"Make sure you continue to take them until you're finished."

"Ok Dr."

"Call again when you need another appointment – I need to see you again before you try and get pregnant."

"Dr. Campana?"

"Yes Trenice?"

"You never answered my question."

"What question was that Trenice?"

"Are you ok?" Dr. Campana picked up 2 pictures of a little boy and a little girl on her desk.

"These are my twins – this is my son Tajourne and this is my daughter Zenzi." Jordan and I walked out of Dr. Campana's office arm in arm, grinning ear to ear. When we opened the door to leave we could hear Dr. Campana yelling at the receptionist, "I said in my office – now!"

Chapter 77

"Hey guys!" Jake said as we walked up to their front door. "What brings you two here?"

"Oh we were just in the neighborhood," Jordan said.

"Yea right," Rachel laughed.

"You two are grinning like two cats that swallowed the Canary – what's up Trenice?"

"Oh nothing..."

"So you just came by to visit – you just happened to be in the neighborhood – and nothing's going on?"

"Well..."

"I knew it! Spit it out or else!" she said as she went to tickle me and I winced in pain.

"Damn Trenice – I'm sorry – you ok?"

"Yea – I'm ok."

"You sure you ok Trenice?" Jake asked. "You need some Tylenol?"

"I need a drink," I laughed. "Comin' right up – you want one babe?"

"Yea," Rachel said. "Trenice you sure you ok?" I didn't mean to hurt you."

"It's okay – actually I couldn't be better."

"Oh? Why's that?"

"Yea – what gives?" Jake asked as he passed Jordan a can of Pepsi and passed Rachel and me a drink of 151 and Pepsi.

"Damn! You sure make a mean drink!" I laughed as I took a sip.

"Uh huh – that shit'll sneak up on ya," Rachel laughed.

"Easy li'l mother – you need to be able to walk to the car," Jordan laughed.

"Oh shut up," I laughed as I finished my drink.

"Damn girl – kinda thirsty?" Rachel laughed.

"I guess I was," I laughed.

"So what's up Trenice?" she asked as she sipped her drink.

"Like I said – I couldn't be better," I said as I laid my head in Jordan's lap and he stroked my hair.

"It sure is nice to see you two so happy again," Jake said.

"Yea – now can you stay that way? Please?" Rachel laughed.

"From your lips to God's ears," Jordan said.

"I can't believe all the drama you two have had – shit you been in drama since you started seeing each other," Rachel laughed.

"I knew Trenice wasn't goin' nowhere when she was ready to take on Rosalind," Jake laughed.

"Damn right!" I hollered.

"Oh she feelin' that drink now!" Rachel laughed.

"Damn right!" I hollered again. They all bust out laughing.

"I was really impressed with the way you stood by your man Trenice - most women would've said 'fuck this."

"Most women don't love Jordan like I do," I said.

"Damn right!" Rachel hollered. We all bust out laughing again.

"I'm serious Trenice – Jordan's a lucky man – hell – he's almost as lucky as me, "Jake laughed.

"So whatchu sayin' man?" Jordan laughed.

"I'm the lucky one – Jordan would've never come to the hospital if it weren't for you two – you could've told him to forget all about me."

"Naa...I knew better than that Trenice," Jake said.

"We both knew better," Rachel said.

"You two remind me of us when we first got together."

"We do?" Jordan and I said in unison.

"Yep. All the shit you've been through would've tore you two apart if you weren't supposed to be together," Rachel said.

"I believe that too...what's so funny honey?" I asked Jordan as he started laughing.

"Just listening to them analyze us," he laughed. "Like they're experts 'n shit."

"Hey – watch it!" Jake laughed.

"So have you heard from Char?" Rachel asked.

"Not since she was at our house last week," I said.

"You think she's mad?"

"I know I would be."

"Why would you be mad Trenice?" Jake asked.

"Well, if I found out Jordan was playin' me with Rosalind – especially when we found out she was pregnant - then I found out he raped my best friend?"

"So you would be mad at Char?"

"Hell no! I'd be mad at myself."

"Why Trenice?" Jordan asked.

"Well, I'd be mad at myself for being so stupid."

"Oh so Char's stupid?"

"That's not what I said!"

"Okay, okay...calm down Trenice!" Jordan said.

"Anyway – I'd be mad at myself for being so stupid and I'd feel like I let my friend down."

"Damn Trenice – you think Char blames herself for what happened to you?" Rachel asked.

"I know she does."

"But she had nothing to do with what happened to you!"

"Sure she does."

"Trenice!"

"Let me finish..."

"Okay."

"Yea – I gotta hear this one too," Jake said.

"Say it was me instead of Char and it was Jordan instead of Cornell..."

"Why it gotta be me Trenice?"

"Let me finish please..."

"Ok – go 'head."

"Well, if I was told over and over to stay away from you and find my own man and I didn't listen – then my best friend ends up gettin' raped – do you think you could convince me it wasn't my fault?"

"I guess not Trenice," Rachel said.

"So what are you gonna do Trenice?" Jake asked.

"I'm gonna leave her alone and give her some time."

"She'll come around Trenice," Jordan said.

"I hope so honey – I miss her a lot."

"Maybe you should call her and tell her that," Rachel said.

"Naa...I think if I call her I'll just be pouring more salt in the would – it's not enough that she found out Cornell was playin' her – she got put on blast by Sissy and now everybody else knows her business 'cause News 12 put it all out!"

"Damn – I forgot all about that shit!" Rachel said.

"I bet she'll think twice before she messes with another married man," Jake laughed.

"Oh boy – you know how Trenice gets when you talk about Char," Jordan said.

"I'm sorry Trenice –no offense intended," Jake said.

"None taken – besides, you're right."

"Huh?" they all said in unison.

"You're right," I said again.

"Damn – I never thought I'd hear you say that Trenice," Jordan said.

"Well its true honey · Char knew he was married from the beginning so she can't really blame News 12 or Sissy."

"I hope she realizes that," Jordan said.

"I don't think she cares about that – I think she cares more about the fact that I continued to sympathize with here and support her even after Cornell raped me. She might even be mad at me for not telling her."

"Are you serious?" Rachel asked.

"Yep."

"Why would she be mad at you for not telling her?" Jordan asked.

"Yea – explain that one," Jake said.

"Well, what if it was me and Jordan in the situation..."

"Here we go..." Jordan said.

"Let her finish!" Jake and Rachel yelled in unison.

"Aiight then – damn!" Jordan laughed.

"I would be mad for the simple fact that if Char had told me she was raped in the beginning, I wouldn't have stayed in the relationship – I would've left him – then I never would have gone to the funeral and my business wouldn't be all over Westchester, thanks to News 12."

"Damn – I never thought of that," Rachel said. "Shit – I might be mad at you too.

"Exactly."

"Well if she thinks about it she'll see why you didn't tell her."

"You just said you might be mad at me Rachel."

"Uh huh," Jordan and Jake said in unison.

"Aiight, aiight – you got me there," Rachel laughed.

"Well, I think you were right not to tell her, "Jordan said.

"Really?" Rachel asked.

"Yea...look at all the stuff Trenice was dealing with at the time – and to top it off – she ends up losing our baby!"

"Don't be so hard on her honey – she was there through everything remember?"

"I'm not being hard on her Trenice – I'm just saying you were going through a lot of shit yourself, so she should understand why you didn't tell her."

"I agree," Jake said.

"Your baby?" We all looked at Rachel in shock without speaking.

"Oh... we never got a chance to tell ya did we?" Jordan said.

"No you didn't!" Jake yelled.

"Well, remember Sissy said she was pregnant?"

"Yea..." they said in unison.

"Well, Char was tryin' to get pregnant."

"Why the fuck would she want his baby?" Rachel asked.

"Same reason I wanted Jordan's baby."

"Oh damn – I forgot – you never told her you were raped – ok – go'head."

"Well Char and I were talkin' and she pointed out the fact that if she was tryin' to get pregnant and couldn't, then how the hell is Sissy pregnant by him?"

"Damn! They both said in unison.

"That's what we said too. After Char went home I kept thinking about what she said."

"I don't get it Trenice. So what Char was tryin' to have his baby. So what she didn't get pregnant. And who cares if Sissy got pregnant by someone else?"

"I didn't get it either Rachel - but keep thinking... it'll come to ya..." Jordan said.

"Hmmm... let's see... Char didn't get pregnant, Sissy got pregnant by someone else...oh damn!"

"'Bout fuckin' time you got it!" Jake said.

"Damn – sorry y'all."

"No need to be sorry Rachel – I didn't get it at first either," Jordan said.

"Y'all gonna try again?"

"Damn Rachel – give 'em a minute!" Jake laughed.

Rachel sat there looking at us for a few seconds then she yelled, "Oh my God – you're pregnant already!"

"Hell no!" Jordan and I both yelled in unison.

"Well why were you two smiling like two cats that swallowed the canary when you got here then?"

"We just left Dr. Campana's office."

"Oh? What she say?"

"She said they told her the same thing they told me."

"Damn Trenice."

"She also told me she got an infection and they had to take her fallopian tube and her ovary."

"Ok I must be stuck on stupid today."

"Why you say that Rachel?"

"The doctor told you that and that made you happy?"

"No Rachel."

"Oh ok – so I'm not stuck on stupid then," she laughed.

"No you're not stuck anywhere," I laughed.

"So why are you two so happy then?"

"Dr. Campana showed us pictures of her twins Tajourne and Zenzi."

"Wait a minute...she got an infection, they took her fallopian tube, and her ovary, and she got pregnant with twins?"

"Yea," Jordan and I said in unison as we looked into each other's eyes.

Chapter 78

"How you show up empty-handed?" Miss April laughed as we walked into the backyard.

"Hey Mum," Jordan said as he kissed his grandmother on the cheek.

"Hi Miss April," I said as I hugged her.

"You don't bring shit, you can't eat shit," Aunt Trudy said.

"What'd you bring Trudy?" Jordan asked sarcastically.

"Sissy on her way back from the store now," Aunt Trudy said.

"Trenice don't pay Trudy no mind – y'all can eat whatever you want," Miss April laughed.

"Damn right!" Jordan said as he handed me a glass of ice tea.

"Why they here anyway?" I whispered to Jordan.

"Cause your grandmother invited them!" Miss June yelled as if I was talking to the entire neighborhood.

"Mum, what's in that glass?" Jordan asked.

"Mind your business Jordan," she laughed.

"Yea, mind your business," Aunt Trudy laughed.

"She wasn't talkin' to you Aunt Trudy!" I yelled.

"Don't let me have to beat your ass again Trenice," she laughed.

"You ain't never beat my ass," I laughed as I sipped my tea.

"Your mother's not here to pull me off of you now Trenice," she said as she started to eat some potato salad of her plate.

"And your mother's not here either," I said as I finished my tea.

"Oh yes I am Trenice!" Grandma said as she walked into the backyard. "Knock it off!"

"As long as she stays over there with her friend, I'll be just fine," I said as I picked up a chicken wing and proceeded to bite it.

"What'd I miss?" Sissy asked as she walked into the backyard with a couple of bottles of Bacardi, a couple of bottles of coke, and two six-pack of Budweiser.

"Oh so I see what Sissy brought – what'd you bring Trudy?" Jordan asked.

"See Ma – that's what the fuck I'm talkin' about!" Aunt Trudy yelled as she got up to throw her plate in the garbage.

"Damn Trudy – you grown – why you gotta call your Mamma?" Jordan laughed.

"Will you two knock it the fuck off!" Grandma yelled.

"Shut up Gladys," Miss June laughed.

"I'm sick of this shit every time we go somewhere!" Grandma yelled.

"So am I – maybe you and Trudy should've stayed home," Miss April said.

"You ain't said nothin' but a word!" Grandma said as she stormed out the backyard.

"Ma! Ma! Where you goin'?" Aunt Trudy yelled as she ran after Grandma.

"Bitch said we should've stayed home – so we're leaving!" she yelled as she tried to snatch Aunt Trudy by the arm.

"Since I'm a bitch you don't have to bring yo' ass back to my house – and make sure you take Trudy with you!" Miss April yelled.

"You lucky that's your grandmother," Jordan said.

"They'll be playin' cards next week," Miss June laughed.

"Trenice what'd you do to your grandmother?" Sissy asked.

"Yea Trenice – what'd you do to Ma?" Aunt Trudy asked.

"I ain't do shit to her – you did," I said.

"Keep poppin' shit Trenice," she said as she came towards me and I stood up.

"Whatchu gon' do?"I asked.

"You know what bitch – I'm sick of you!" she yelled as she slapped me back into the fence, causing me to drop my plate of food.

"What the fuck..." Jordan tried to get in between us but I was too mad and too quick...

"Jordan get her!" Miss April yelled as I came off the fence with a left hook, knocking Aunt Trudy to the ground. I jumped on top of her and continued punching and pulling while she was simultaneously punching and pulling on me.

"Oh hell no!" Sissy yelled as she came running to break of the fight, but Jordan got there first...

"Oh no you not!" he yelled as he snatched her back away from us.

"Oooooooeeeeeeee!" Miss June laughed. "Evil blood runs deep and these two sure have their Daddy's temper!" That stopped us dead in our fight...

"Whatchu say?" We asked in unison.

"Nothing... never mind..." she mumbled.

"You need to leave Trudy," Miss April said as she tried to take Trudy by the arm.

"How you know?" Aunt Trudy asked.

"You talk too much – especially when you drink June," Miss April said. "Trudy – I said you need to leave – now!"

"C'mon Sissy," Aunt Trudy snapped. "Shit done hit the fan!" she said as they left.

"Mum – what's going on?" Jordan asked.

"Leave it alone Jordan," Miss April said.

"Oh no I will not leave it alone either," I said as I walked over to Jordan's mother. "What did you say?" I asked her point blank.

"I thought you knew," she mumbled.

"You thought I knew what?" I asked. Jordan sat down with his head in his hands. Miss April made herself a plate of food, poured herself some tea, and sat down.

"Don't stop now June, Miss April said between forkfuls. "Tell her."

"I thought you knew that Thomas was your father," Miss June said with her head down.

"Thomas? Thomas Johnson? Me and my mother have the same father? Neil isn't my father?" I asked.

"No, No, No... you and Trudy have the same father," Miss June said.

"Aunt Trudy knew?" I asked.

"Yea she knew," Miss June answered.

"How you know Mum?" Jordan asked.

"Gladys told us," Miss April said.

"And you told Trudy?" Jordan yelled.

"We ain't tell Trudy shit – Gladys told her!" Miss April yelled.

"Unfuckinbelieveable!" Jordan yelled.

"Watch your mouth son," Miss June said.

"I wish you'd a watched yours," Jordan said sarcastically.

"Don't you ever disrespect your mother!" Miss April said as she got up to slap Jordan but I saw her coming and stepped in between them. "Move Trenice."

"No I'm not," I said as I grabbed her into a hug.

"Let me go Trenice," she laughed.

"Sure Miss April," I laughed. "I'll let you go right over there and make us a plate of food 'cause we did come to eat," I laughed as I let her go.

"Y'all can get your own damn food," she laughed as she sat back down. "And bring me some tea while you're at it!" she laughed.

"So when did my mother find out Neil wasn't my father?" I asked.

"You need to ask your mother Trenice," Miss June said.

218

"Oh, now she need to ask her mother," Jordan said as he rolled his eyes. "Here Mum," he said as he handed Miss April another glass of tea.

"Honey, you need help?" I asked as I got up to help him make the plates for us.

"I got it," he said.

"Let me help you, 'cause you movin' kind of slow and I'm hungry," I laughed.

"Here – take your plate," he laughed as he handed it to me.

"Here – take your tea," I laughed as I placed it in front of him.

"I guess you are hungry – I'd be hungry too after fighting like that with my sister," Miss June laughed.

"We may have the same daddy – but that bitch will NEVER be my sister!" I laughed.

"Damn right!" Jordan laughed as we ate potato salad, baked macaroni & cheese, collard greens, fried chicken wings, and grilled shrimp.

Chapter 79

"What took y'all so long? Did you forget I was coming over?" Char asked as we walked up to the front of our building.

"Sorry Char – how long were you waiting?" I asked as we went inside.

"About an hour," she said.

"Sorry you waited so long," Jordan said.

"Oh that's okay – I didn't mind – I had lunch with Carl while I was waiting."

"Carl?" we both asked in unison.

"Yes, Carl – why?" she asked.

"Never mind – c'mon inside," Jordan said as we went inside and closed the door.

"So what'd you have for lunch?" I asked.

"Cut the shit Trenice – what happened?" Char asked.

"You already know," Jordan laughed.

"Again?" Char asked.

"Again!" Jordan laughed.

"Who invited them anyway?" Char asked.

"My grandmother," I answered.

"How she gonna invite them to somebody else's house?" Char asked.

"Who knows?" Jordan laughed. "But my grandmother told Gladys maybe they should have stayed home," Jordan laughed.

"Then Damn – what'd I miss?" Char asked.

"That's the same question Sissy had when she came back from the store," Jordan laughed.

"She was there too? Why was she... Oh... never mind..."

"She bought the liquor!" we all said in unison as we bust out laughing.

"So why your grandmother told them they should have stayed home?" Char asked.

"Soon as we got there Miss April asked us how we show up empty handed, so Aunt Trudy gon' say you don't bring shit you can't eat shit."

"How the fuck she running a cook out in somebody else's house?" Char asked.

"Exactly!" Jordan said. "I asked her what she bring and she gon' say Sissy on her way back from the store."

"So she ain't bring shit either," Char laughed.

"Exactly!" Jordan laughed. "Plus, my grandmother told us don't pay her any mind."

"She didn't need to tell y'all that!" Char laughed.

"You right!" I laughed.

"My mother was feelin' a lil' tipsy so I asked her what was in her glass – she told me to mind my business, so here go Trudy talkin' 'bout yea, mind your business," Jordan laughed.

"I wish I was there – I would'a told her mind her fuckin' business!" Char said.

"I wish you were there too – so you could've seen Trenice on that ass!" Jordan laughed.

"Damn – I missed it?" Char screamed.

"Did you ever!" Jordan yelled.

"What the hell happened Trenice?" Char yelled.

"When she told Jordan to mind his business, I said she wasn't talkin' to you Aunt Trudy, so she talkin' 'bout don't let me have to beat your ass again!" I laughed.

"Why she keep sayin' she beat your ass? She ain't never beat your ass!" Char yelled.

"That's what Trenice told her," Jordan laughed.

"Yea – she gon' say your mother's not here to pull me off of you so I said neither is yours – that's when my grandmother shows up talkin' about knock it off," I said.

"How she just gon' walk in there tellin' you to knock it off – she don't even know what happened!" Char said.

"I told her as long as Aunt Trudy stays over there with her friend I'll be fine," I laughed.

"So Sissy walks in with the liquor and I said oh I see what Sissy brought – what did you bring Trudy – so she gon' get mad talkin' 'bout see Ma that's what the fuck I'm talkin' about, so I said damn you grown – why you gotta call your Mama?" Jordan laughed.

"Oooohhh I know she was mad!" Char laughed.

"So Gladys gon' tell us both to knock it the fuck off and my mother told her to shut up!" Jordan laughed.

"Oooohhh shit!" Char yelled.

"Yea – then she gon' say she sick of this shit every time they go somewhere, so Miss April said so am I - maybe you and Trudy should've stayed home," I laughed.

"Wow," Char laughed.

"Oh it gets better," Jordan laughed. "Gladys told my grandmother you ain't said nothing but a word and storms out the backyard, then Trudy starts yellin' Ma! Ma!" Jordan laughed again. "Then she has the nerve to tell Trudy, bitch said maybe we should'a stayed home so we're leaving, so my grandmother told her since I'm a bitch you don't have to bring your ass back to my house and make sure you take Trudy with you! I told Trenice she lucky that's her grandmother."

"I know that's right – how she gonna call your grandmother a bitch?"Char said.

"My mother thought it was funny – she said they'll be playing cards next week – but I didn't like that shit." Jordan said.

"I don't like that shit either." Char said.

"So now here come Sissy askin' me what did I do to my grandmother, then Aunt Trudy coming right behind her askin' what'd I do to Ma – so I told her I didn't do shit to her – you did!" I said.

"Oh I know she didn't like that shit!" Char said.

"She didn't – she gon' tell me keep poppin' shit so I stood up and said whatchu gon' do, then she slapped me so hard I fell against the fence and dropped my plate of food," I said.

"Oh hell no! Jordan you let Trudy hit Trenice and you ain't do shit... oh wait... never mind... I forgot the funeral – what happened next Trenice?" Char asked.

"I jumped up off that fence with a left hook and knocked that bitch down – that's what the fuck happened," I laughed.

"My girl!" Char yelled as she high-5ed me.

"Ouch!" I said is I tried to put my arm higher.

"You aiight Trenice? Char asked.

"Hell yea I'm aiight – I'm just a little sore," I said.

"Y'all was fightin' like that?" Char asked.

"Hell yea – when she fell down, I fell right on top of her and commenced to punching!" I yelled, "But she was getting' her's in too," I laughed.

"Who stopped you from fighting" Char asked.

"My mother," Jordan answered.

"Your mother?" Char asked.

"Yea," Jordan said.

"Oh I gotta hear this one," Char said.

"So we're down there fightin' and Miss June gon' start laughin' talkin' 'bout evil blood runs deep and these two sure have their daddy's temper," I said.

"Whatchu mean y'all have your daddy's temper?" Char asked.

"My grandmother told Trudy to leave, but Trudy and her dumb ass turns around and asks my mother how she know," Jordan said.

"How she know what?" Char asked.

"How does she know that we have the same father Char," I answered.

"Wait... so Neil isn't your father?" Char asked.

"Nope." I answered.

"So you and your mother have the same father?" Char asked.

"Nope. Just me and Trudy – and Trudy knew it all this time."

"I wonder who told her?" Char asked.

"Gladys did," Jordan said.

"What the fuck is wrong with them?" Char asked.

"Hell if I know," Jordan answered.

"Miss June said she thought I knew, Miss April told her she talk too much, Jordan said it was unfuckinbelievable, Miss June told him to watch his mouth, he told her he wish she'd watch her mouth, then Miss April gets up like she gon' slap him talkin' 'bout don't you ever disrespect your mother," I said angrily.

"I don't believe this shit!" Char said. Your mother never said anything to you?

"Nope." I answered.

"So did she hit you Jordan?" Char asked.

"She was about to, but Trenice had my back," Jordan laughed.

"Trenice! You hit his grandmother?" Char asked.

"Girl I ain't crazy!" I laughed. "I grabbed her into a hug and when she told me to let go I told her sure I'ma let you go over there and make us a plate of food," I laughed.

"Girl, you ARE crazy!" Char laughed. What'd she do?

"She sat down and told us we could get our own damn food, so we did!" Jordan laughed.

"So what'd you have for lunch?" Char laughed.

"You first!" Jordan and I said in unison as we all laughed.

.

Chapter 80

"I'll be back in about an hour Beautiful," Jordan said as he closed the door behind him.

"Might as well see what's going on the the world," I said as I turned on News 12 and sat down...

"We interrupt our regularly scheduled programming to bring you this latest bulletin from News 12. News 12 has just determined that the 2nd body that was blown up in the explosion in White Plains some weeks ago has been identified as Thomas Johnson. News 12 has also determined that Cornell Jones, who was also blown up in the explosion, was Thomas Johnson's son. Thomas Johnson was incarcerated for armed robbery and murder back in June 1979. He was paroled earlier this year long with his son, Cornell Jones. It has not yet been determined why Cornell Jones and his father, Thomas Johnson, were in the gas station together, but the coroner has determined that Thomas Johnson's body had been there for quite some time due to the decomposition of the body. We have yet to determine whether Cornell Jones was responsible for the death of his father, Thomas Johnson, but News 12 has determined that they were both paroled at the same time. We now continue with our regularly scheduled programming."

"Hmff - just when I find out who my father really is I find out he's dead," I laughed. "Oh well no biggie I guess – besides, I have a real father – pain in the ass, drunk off his ass bastard, beat the shit out of my mother then we jumped his ass and beat the shit outta him...oh my God – I don't believe this shit – wait 'till I tell Jordan – he's probably gonna wonder what the fuck I'm laughing at... ha ha ha ha ha... – hell – I don't even know what the fuck I'm laughing at!" I hollered as I continued to laugh so hard I was holding my stomach... "Wooo eee – my real father was an armed robber and a murderer, and my Daddy's a no good drunk ass bastard – and Mommy had the nerve to say somethin' 'bout Torbett – if that ain't the muthafuckin' pot callin' the muthafuckin' kettle purple!" I hollered as I went into the kitchen to pour myself some kiwi lemonade... "Yea I can't wait to tell Jordan this one – I wonder if Aunt Trudy's seen News 12 today – ha ha ha ha ha... I wonder if Grandma's seen News 12 – tee hee hee hee hee – bet neither one of 'em 'll have shit to say to me now," I laughed as I drank the lemonade and put the glass in the sink. "Le'me tell Char this one," I laughed as I sat down at the dining room table and dialed her number... "Shit... busy... figures... who the fuck she talkin' too –

don't she know I got gossip?" I laughed as I hung up the phone and went into the bedroom. Then it hit me… like a ton of bricks… "Wait a minute… Thomas Johnson was my father… Cornell Jones was his son… Oh God noooooooooooooo!" I screamed as I fell down onto the floor, pulled my knees up to my chest, and began rocking back and forth uncontrollably. "Not my own brother! Oh God · my brother raped me… and I killed him! Why God – whyyyyyyyyyyyyyyy?" I screamed as I continued to rock back and forth. I snatched open the bottom drawer to the night stand, snatched out a pad and pencil, and began scribbling…

"If I knew before hand, would I still be here?"

"If I had a choice would I still be here?"

"If only I knew when it started – maybe I could have prevented it…"

"If only I knew what to change –maybe I could've changed it…"

"If I knew what to change would I want to change or would I ask why can't you accept the real me?"

"If I knew this was pre-determined before I was born would I still want to be born?"

"If I have to spend the rest of my life feeling this way do I want to live it?"

"It's understandable when lies work · but what if you're the only one who believes them?"

"How do you stop believing the worst when the worst is all you get?"

"If you have no one to talk to but your soul mate and your soul mate isn't here – what do you do?"

I snatched the paper off the pad, crumbled it up, threw it across the room, broke the pencil in half, threw both pieces across the room, grabbed my knees up to my chest, and started rocking back and forth again...

Chapter 81

"Where's Jordan when I need him?" I cried out loud. "Oh God – please make the pain go away – I can't take it anymore!" I got up off the floor and ran to the bathroom... "Shit, Dammit, Muthafucka!" I yelled as I threw the empty bottle of Tylenol on the floor. I ran into the kitchen, snatched open the bottom cabinet, and grabbed the ½ gallon of Bacardi 151. "Now that's what I'm talkin' about!" I yelled as I started guzzling the Bacardi... "Damn this shit is nasty!" I laughed as I continued to drink... "Ooooooeeeee..... I ain't feelin' shit now!" I laughed as I finished the ½ gallon. I sat there for a few minutes just allowing the feeling of numbness to take over. When I started to feel like I was going to vomit any second, I laughed as I tried to get up and slumped back down on the floor. "Oh well... tee hee hee... I guess I'll... wait until... Jordan... gets... home... he...

can... carry... me... to the... bathroom... he... can... zzzzz..." The next thing I knew I was looking down at myself on the kitchen floor. I was lying in a pool of my own vomit mixed with blood and I wasn't moving. "Damn – I fucked up," I cried as I continued to look down at my body. I watched as Jordan came in looking for me.

"Trenice? Trenice? You hidin' from me?" I watched in agony for us both as he went to the living room, the dining room, the bathroom, and then the bedroom. "I'm over here Jordan!" I yelled as if he could hear me.

"She musta went out – I told her I'd be right back – oh well, might as well put this stuff away," he said as he came towards the kitchen.

"He'll find me now," I said as he went towards the refrigerator, humming along as he opened the refrigerator and started putting things away. "Hurry up Jordan!" I yelled as he moved to the cabinets on the other side of the table...

"Damn – what the hell is that smell? Where is it coming from? Oh my God – Trenice – what'd you go and do this for?" he cried as he cradled me in his arms... "Trenice wake up baby –please wake up," he cried as he dialed 911.

"I can't Jordan, I can't!" I cried as I watched him cradle my body against his.

"She won't wake up!" he cried into the phone. "I don't know! I don't know! Ok hurry – please wake up baby," he cried as he hung up the phone. I cried along with him as I listened to the sirens.

"God I wish I could feel you holding me. I wish I could wake up and be with you,' I cried as they kicked down the door.

"Sir Where are you?"

"I'm here!"

"Sir let go..."

"I can't..."

"We need to get her to the hospital – now let her go!"

"Get the fuck off me!"

"C'mon – you can ride in the ambulance but let us do our job ok?" the other tech said as Jordan stepped aside. "What happened? Did she overdose?" Jordan didn't say anything. He just picked up the empty bottle of Bacardi and handed it to them along with the empty bottle of Tylenol. I watched as they hoisted my body up onto the gurney, strapped me onto it, and flew out the door. Jordan was right on their heels as the door slammed in my face.

"Dammit! How the fuck am I supposed to get outta here?!" I yelled. "Oh shit – I forgot..." I said as I walked through the door and floated downstairs to the ambulance. "Shit – they're pulling off – I gotta get in there!" Just when I got to the back door, they hit a pothole and got stuck for about two seconds – just what I needed to get in the ambulance. "So that's what potholes are for...Thank you Lord." At least he could hear me.

"Is she an alcoholic?"

"No."

"Why would she try and kill herself?"

"She didn't."

"Sir, you just gave me an empty bottle..."

"Didn't I just tell you she didn't try and kill herself?"

"Okay – what happened?"

"I don't know."

"Was she okay earlier?"

"Yes."

"How long were you gone?"

"About two hours."

"And she was fine when you left?

"Yes."

"Was she drinking?"

"No!"

"Sir, I'm just trying to find out what happened..."

"I don't know what the fuck happened! Trenice wake up – please don't leave me..."

"I can't wake up honey," I said as I cried on his shoulder.

"Don't cry Trenice, don't cry – you're gonna be ok...

"Trenice? Is that her name?"

"Yes – Trenice Robertson."

"Sir, she's out cold – she's not crying."

"Yes she is."

"See for yourself."

"I don't need to see her."

"What do you mean?"

"I can hear her."

"Poor man is so confused he doesn't know what he's saying," the other tech mumbled.

"I'm not confused – I can hear her crying."

"Well if you can hear her crying, why won't she wake up then?" he asked sarcastically.

"Because she can't," he said as he took my hand.

"Your name sir?"

"Jordan Williams."

"What's your relationship to Trenice?"

"I'm her husband." I followed them out of the ambulance into St. Joseph's emergency room. As luck would have it, we ran right into Aunt Trudy.

"Oh my God – what happened? Trenice wake up – wake up!" she yelled as she slapped my face on the left and on the right.

"We have an overdose here," the tech yelled out.

"I told you she didn't try and kill herself dammit!" Jordan yelled.

"Sir, we have an overdose whether she tried to kill herself or not – step back please.

"Jordan why don't you..."

"I'm not going anywhere Trudy!"

"I was gonna say sit down over here – I'll come get you when she's stable."

"Ok," Jordan said as he sat down. I watched as my body was thrown from the gurney to the bed, tubes were stuck in my hands, my arms, my nose, and down my throat...

"She's not responding Dr..."

"Noooooooooo!" Jordan screamed and ran towards the bed...

"Jordan go sit down!" I yelled as if he could hear me. Aunt Trudy must've heard me 'cause she ran right up to him...

"Jordan, let them take care of her..."she said as they wheeled me down the hall and the doors closed behind me.

"Get the fuck off me!" he yelled as he pushed her away from him...

"Jordan they'll throw you out if you don't calm down..."

"Is there a problem here Trudy?" Roy said.

"Naa...I got this Roy..."

"Well let me know if he gives you any trouble..."

"Yo man shut the fuck up robo cop!" Jordan yelled.

"You wanna piece a me?" Roy asked as he started to walk towards Jordan.

"Roy go sit your old ass down for you fall down," Aunt Trudy laughed. Jordan and I laughed right along with her.

"Shit – I may be old but he can't do shit!"

"Aiight man – it's all good – I'm aiight..." Jordan said.

"You better be..." Roy said as he went back down the hall.

"Old as muthafucka – who he talking too?" Jordan laughed.

"Jordan shut up 'fore he go get the police – what happened anyway?"

"I don't know."

"Jordan you gotta know something..."

"I said I don' know what the fuck happened – don't you think if I knew I would tell them – damn!"

"You right...but..."

"But what?"

"Y'all was drinkin'? Partyin'?"

"No!"

"Well how she drunk then?"

"I left to go to Shoprite. I was gone for two hours. I came back from Shoprite and I called her. She didn't answer me so I looked in the living room, the bedroom, and the bathroom. I saw the empty bottle of Tylenol on the floor but I didn't see her so I figured she musta went out – so I went into the kitchen to put the food away..." Aunt Trudy put her hand on Jordan's shoulder as he started crying. I went around the chair and hugged him from behind and cried with him. "Trenice is crying again."

"Again? Did you have a fight or something?"

"No."

"So how do you know she's crying?" And what do you mean again?"

"Nothing – forget it!"

"Jordan tell me!"

"Aiight but I don't wanna hear no shit."

"Ok, ok – just tell me what the fuck is going on!" Aunt Trudy's concern shocked us both.

"When I found Trenice on the floor in the kitchen, she was laying in her own vomit."

"That's good."

"What the fuck? How is that good?"

"She has alcohol poisoning. If she didn't throw up she'd be dead."

"What?!"

"Yea...anytime someone overdoses..."

"She didn't..."

"Leme finish..."

"Ok."

"Anytime someone overdoses, the 1st thing we do is pump the stomach. 99% of the time they turn out ok, but if Trenice took the Tylenol and then drank the liquor she was tryin' to commit suicide – that means we gotta put her on suicide watch for 24 hours, then she'll get a psychological evaluation. She might even be committed to Hall 2 upstairs."

"Ain't nobody committing Trenice to the psych ward – fuck that!"

"Jordan it's the best thing..."

"I should'a known what you were up to bitch – you'd like that wouldn't you?"

"Jordan you're not stupid – the cops are already askin' questions – everybody thinks you're her husband – you sign her in – you come back in 24 hours – you sign her out – end of story."

"You have a point – I can't believe I actually agree with you for once," he laughed.

"Damn I wish Trenice would wake up," Aunt Trudy said.

"She can't. That's why she's crying."

"You sure you ain't been drinkin'?"

"I wasn't drinkin'. When I found her in the kitchen I tried to wake her up. She started cryin' 'cause she can't wake up. I tried to tell them the same thing in the ambulance but they think I'm confused."

"Well..."

"I don't give a damn what anyone thinks – I know she's here and I heard her crying."

"Trudy where is she? What happened to my baby?" I went over to my mother and hugged her as she cried.

"Your baby has alcohol poisoning or..."

"Don't fuckin' say it Trudy!" Jordan yelled.

"Say what? What's going on Trudy?" Grandma asked.

"We don't know Ma. Trenice came in the ambulance – Jordan gave them an empty bottle of Tylenol and an empty bottle of Bacardi."

"Trenice didn't try and commit suicide Trudy," my mother said.

"What makes you so sure Claire?"

"Trudy don't be so damn stupid – you know damn well Trenice didn't try and commit suicide!" Grandma yelled.

"Thank you Miss Gladys," Jordan said. "I'ma go get some coffee – y'all want some?"

"Yea Jordan – bring us back some coffee…" When Aunt Trudy was sure Jordan was gone she said, "Ma, something's wrong."

"We know that Trudy."

"I'm serious Ma."

"Wattchu mean?"

"He says he can hear her cryin' Ma."

"Yea? So?"

"How can he hear her cryin' if she's unconscious?"

"Remember when I had my heart attack last year?"

"Yea?"

"The doctors told you I died and they brought me back right?"

"Yea."

"I heard you cryin' too."

"You did?"

"Yea I did. And I saw you holding my hand too."

"You saw me Ma?"

"Yea I saw you. And Claire."

"Where were you Ma?"my mother asked.

"I was standing behind you and Trudy, Claire. I helped you find your wallet too."

"Oh my God – I remember that – I was going crazy looking for my wallet! I couldn't remember where I put it! Then all of a sudden – out of nowhere – I remembered I left it in the glove compartment!"

"No Claire – I reminded you," my grandmother said.

"Reminded who?" Jordan asked as he brought them their coffee. "Here Trudy."

"Oh you got me coffee too? Le'me find out...thanks."

"You're welcome."

"Ma was telling me she reminded me where I put my wallet last year when she had her heart attack."

"You had a heart attack Miss Gladys?"

"Yea – I had one last year. And I heard Trudy cryin' just like you hear Trenice cryin'. If she tried to kill herself she wouldn't be cryin' 'cause she can't wake up." Jordan didn't say anything. He just sat down and smiled. I was smiling too.

"Go 'head with your bad self Grandma," I said.

While they continued drinking their coffee and talking, I had other problems... all of a sudden, in the middle of their conversations, I was 'pulled' through the double doors that closed behind me. Once behind the double doors, I saw 3 rooms with 3 glass windows on each room. All I could see from where I was standing was 3 white sheets over 3 bodies so I 'flew' over the the windows to find out which body was mine.

"Shit – Ceila at it again – I guess they'll just let her sleep it off," I laughed as I looked in the 1st room.

"Damn – what the fuck happened to his head?" I said as I saw the doctors scurrying back and forth while I looked in the 2nd room. "He's lost a lot of blood – we gotta close the wound quickly," the doctor said as they worked on his head.

"What the fuck happened to him anyway?" the nurse asked?"

"Same ole same ole – went out drinkin' – got in a fight – got his head bashed open with a bottle," the doctor said while sewing his head.

"He's not gonna be able to take much more of this," the nurse said as she handed the doctor the syringe.

"This happens one more time it just might kill him," The doctor said as he closed his head, cleaned up the blood, patched him up, and left to go on to the next one. It amazed me how they do their jobs and carry on conversations while they work – they were so nonchalant but so accurate. I followed the doctor to the 3rd room and that's when I saw myself lying under the sheet.

"Well, well – who have we here?" he asked as he looked at my chart. "Ah… so you're Trenice eh?" he asked as he took the sheet down to my waist, exposing my bare breasts. Why was I naked anyway? Where the hell was my gown? I got a sickening feeling in my stomach as I saw the doctor look out the windows of the room then pull the curtain… "You sure are a pretty girl," he said as he picked up my right hand and kissed it. "This shouldn't hurt – I'll be gentle," he said as he stuck the needle in my hand and hooked me up to an IV. "You poor thing – I'd kiss you if you didn't have that tube down your throat," he said as he placed my right arm down beside me in the bed.

"Oh my God – somebody help me!" I screamed as if someone could hear me.

"You don't look too comfortable – let me adjust your pillow so you don't wake up with a sore neck," he said as he adjust the pillow under my head, then ran his hand down my left arm.

"Don't you touch me you sick twisted fuck!" I screamed as he pulled the sheet down further to my knees, exposing my naked body.

"You're so beautiful," he said as kissed me on my neck.

"Get the fuck off me! I'll kill you!" I screamed.

"Oh God – please don't let him do this to me!"

"Dr. Aiden you finished with her yet?" Roy said as he interrupted him.

"Thank you Jesus!" I yelled as Dr. Aiden jumped up and turned around.

"Just about... whoever put this IV in wrapped it between her legs – I had to take her gown off and redo her IV," he lied.

"Well put her gown on and get her down to suicide watch ⁃ they need this room for the car accident victim," Roy said as he walked away.

"Shit – that was a close one – good thing I had on this lab coat or he would've seen everything – I've gotta be more careful," he said as he put my gown on, re-did the IV, tied my hands and feet to the bedposts, and covered me with the sheet again. I looked in the corner of the room and saw the security camera in the ceiling.

"Guess again motherfucker," I growled.

"Dr Aiden we need this room – she ready to go?"

"She's ready – I'll take her down there now," he said.

"I'll take her – we need you here to attend to the car accident victim," Roy said as he wheeled me out the double doors and into the suicide watch room. Once I was situated, he went back into his booth as the 1st doctor came out the double doors.

"Are you here for Trenice?"

"Yea – what's wrong doctor?" Jordan asked.

"She'll be ok – she's lucky you found her when you did."

"Will she wake up anytime soon?"

"She'll wake up – she'll have one hell of a hangover though – it's actually better she's not awake right now with all the tubes in her. Her throats gonna hurt and she may feel like shit for a couple of days 'cause we had to pump her stomach."

"Thank God!" Jordan yelled.

"Did she have any Tylenol in her stomach?"

"Trudy!" Grandma yelled.

"You just can't leave well enough alone can you?" my mother said.

"Well Claire – if she did you might as well know now…"

"No she didn't," the doctor said.

"I knew damn well Trenice wasn't tryin' to kill herself!" Jordan yelled.

"We all knew it," my mother said.

"When can she go home?" Jordan asked.

"She can't go home until we find out what happened."

"But you already know what happened! She got drunk!"

"We won't know what happened until she can wake up and tell us herself. Until then, she'll be on suicide watch until she wakes up."

"Suicide watch?" Jordan asked.

"Procedure. Someone has to sit in the room with her for tonight. When she wakes up tomorrow, if she's ok, she can go home."

"I'll sit with her tonight," Jordan said.

"That's fine – but you'll have company."

"I'll have company?"

"Yea – the rooms are monitored with cameras by security."

"Fine with me – y'all wanna watch me pick my nose and scratch my ass that's cool – long as I can be with Trenice."

Aunt Trudy, my mother, and my grandmother all bust out laughing along with the doctor.

"Jordan you are sick!" my mother laughed.

"Why you think he gets along with Trenice, Claire?" Grandma laughed.

"Well, my shift is over so I'ma go – see y'all later," Aunt Trudy said.

"We might as well go home too Claire," Grandma said.

"Might as well," my mother yawned.

"Goodnight," Jordan said.

"Good morning," they all yawned as they left the emergency room. I followed Jordan as he went to the room where I was. I watched him touch my head and smooth my hair back.

"Wake up Beautiful...it's time for you to come home."

244

"I can't wake up honey...I'm too tired," I said with tears in my eyes as I watched him untie my wrists from the bed.

"Sir, you can't do that!" Jordan turned around to face Roy.

"Why not? Where's she going?"

"It's just procedure."

"Man, you lookin' right at us – we ain't goin' nowhere – damn!"

"Aiight – but don't tell them I saw you do that – I could lose my job."

"Shit – you know what? Le'me tie her wrists back like they was – it's not like she's awake anyway," he said as he tied my wrists back to the bed. I watched as he turned on the television and sat back in the chair.

"We interrupt our regularly scheduled programming to bring you this latest bulletin from News 12. News 12 has just determined that the 2nd body that was blown up in the explosion in White Plains some weeks ago has been identified as Thomas Johnson. News 12 has also determined that Cornell Jones, who was also blown up in the explosion, was Thomas Johnson's son. Thomas Johnson was incarcerated for armed robbery and murder back in June 1979. He was paroled earlier this year long with his son, Cornell Jones. It has not yet been determined why Cornell Jones and his father, Thomas Johnson, were in the gas station together, but the coroner has determined that Thomas Johnson's body had been there for quite some time due to the decomposition of the body. We have yet to determine whether Cornell Jones was responsible for the death of his father, Thomas Johnson, but News 12 has determined that they were both paroled at the same time. We now continue with our regularly scheduled programming."

"Oh my God..." Jordan whispered. "Trenice was raped by her own brother!"

I continued to watch as Jordan cried on my shoulder.

"I won't let anyone hurt you again Trenice – I swear on my life – no one's ever gonna hurt you again!"

I went over to Jordan, put my arms around him, and lay my head on his back as he continued to cry on my shoulder.

"Don't cry baby – please don't cry," I said as I started crying too.

"Don't cry Trenice – I'm here baby – I'm here...you'll see me when you wake up."

"I see you now Jordan – I wish you could see me too..."

"Yo man – she gonna be aiight?"

"Yea man she'll be aiight," Jordan told Roy.

"Can't stand to be away from her can ya?"

"Hurts like hell."

"She'll be up in a few hours – then the hell will be over man."

"More like it's just beginning..."

"What?"

"Nothin'...never mind..."

"Aiight – le'me get back out here then."

I changed the channel and continued to watch us both as I slept in the bed with my wrists tied down and Jordan slept in the chair.

Chapter 82

Aunt Trudy came into the room with us at 8:00 a.m.

"Damn – she ain't up yet?"

"Nope."

"She must really be tired – le'me go get the doctor."

"Ok Trudy."

"She still asleep?"

"Yea Doc."

"We'll wait another hour – if she's not up by then..."

"Then what?" Jordan asked.

"Let's wait and see," he said as he walked away..."

"Damn – I wonder if she got drunk 'cause she found out I knew she was my sister..."

"Oh please…" I slurred…

"Trenice!" Jordan yelled.

"Yes?"

"You're awake!"

"Yea I'm awake – oh God – I feel like I've been run over by a truck…"

"You're in the hospital Trenice."

"Aunt Trudy?"

"Yea?"

"How long I been here?"

"Since yesterday."

"Damn – I been here all night?"

"Yea – why you get so drunk?"

"Dammit Trudy – can she breathe a minute?" Jordan yelled.

"I was thirsty," I laughed.

"You lucky you know."

"Jordan, untie me."

"Le'me go get the doctor Trenice," Aunt Trudy said.

"Ok."

"You scared me Beautiful," Jordan said as he gave me a kiss.

"I'm sorry," I said as I started to cry.

"Don't cry Trenice – I promise – no one will ever hurt you again…"

"I know… you won't let anyone hurt me again…"

"You heard me?"

"You heard me didn't you?"

"I knew you didn't try to kill yourself…"

"I know."

"How you know Trenice?"

"I was here."

"I know that Trenice."

"No Jordan – I was here. I saw everything. I heard everything. I put my arms around you when you cried on my shoulder."

"I heard you crying…"

"I know, I know…" I said as we hugged, kissed, and cried together…

"I wanted you to wake up so bad…"

"I wanted to wake up and feel your arms around me…"

"I love you soo much – don't ever leave me again…"

"I won't ever leave you again Jordan…I promise…"

"Welcome back Trenice," the doctor said as he came into the room.

"Thanks doctor."

"You're very lucky you know…"

"So I've been told."

"My name is Dr. Johnson. I need to ask you a few questions then, if all goes well, you can go home."

"Whatchu mean if?"

"It'll just take a few minutes."

"Ok."

"So are you suicidal?"

"No."

"So why did you try and kill yourself?"

"I didn't."

"Trenice – I need you to be straight with me…"

"Man what the fuck did she just tell you?"

"Sir I'm gonna have to ask you to leave…"

"No Dr. – I'm asking you to leave – now!" I yelled.

"Fine then!" he yelled as he slammed the door.

"Here Trenice – put your clothes on – let's get the fuck outta here," Jordan said as he handed me my clothes.

"Trenice you leavin? Did you talk to the Dr.?"

"Yea Trudy – she spoke to that jack ass!"

"Who?"

"Dr. Johnson."

"Yea he is an ass – he gets on my fuckin' nerves too... just make sure you sign out before you leave..." Aunt Trudy said.

"Why? They scared I'm gonna sue them?" I laughed.

"Exactly," she said.

"Miss you can't leave until you see the doctor..." the nurse said.

"I've already seen Dr. Johnson." I said.

"Ok then – as soon as he give me the word..."

"I'm giving you the word..." I said.

"Miss I can't let you leave..." the nurse said.

"You can't stop me either..." I said as I got up and started walkin' towards the door.

"Miss Robertson?" Dr. Johnson interrupted.

"Yes?"

"Here are your discharge papers – sign here..."

"Buy bye!" I said sarcastically to the clerk as I signed the papers.

"Miss Robertson, take this card – call them if you ever feel..."

"Sure I will Doc," I said with a smirk as I tossed the card in the garbage.

"What was that Trenice?"

"The number for the suicide hotline," I laughed as Jordan and I walked through the exit.

"Wait here Jordan," I said as I started walking back towards the security booth.

"Where you goin' Trenice? You forgot something?"

"Yea – I'll be right back honey," I said as I kept going towards the booth. When I got there, I saw someone else sitting in the booth.

"Can I help you?" "Yes – I'm looking for Roy," I said.

"He just left – he'll be back on tonight – can I help?"

"No – I need to speak to Roy – it's important…"

"Leme see if I can get him – hang on…" he said as he reached for his walkie talkie…

"Roy ‧ if you're still in the building – please report to the security booth immediately – Roy – if you're still in the building – please report to the security booth immediately."

"I'm half way out the door – what's wrong now?" Roy replied back.

"Someone askin' for you at the booth – she says it's important…"

"Shit – can't it wait until tonight?"

"She says it's important Roy…"

"Who is it?" "Tell him it's Trenice!" I yelled.

"You know Trenice?"

"Trenice? I don't know nobody named Trenice man – I'm out…"

"Tell him Trenice was in the suicide watch room last night…" I pleaded.

"Roy – she says she was in the suicide watch room last night…"

"Oh ok – I'll be right there then…"

"Thank you, thank you, thank you…" I sighed.

"You're welcome – you must be somethin' special – once Roy leaves he don't come back for shit," he laughed.

"Ok I'm back – what's so important?" Roy snapped.

"Yea – what's so important?" Jordan mocked.

"Did you erase the security tapes from last night yet?"

"I just started recording over them,"

"Wait!" I yelled.

"What's going on Trenice?" Roy asked.

"Don't record over the tapes yet – you need to review them so you can see what happened last night!"

"Yo Jim – put the other tapes in man – we can record your shift on those extra tapes while we review the tapes from last night," Roy said.

"Yo – you just gonna take her word for this – what kinda..."

"Don't make me write you up Jim – just do it!" Jim looked at me, rolled his eyes, and stopped recording.

"Yes sir – anything you say sir!" he said sarcastically as he popped out the tapes from last night and popped in fresh tapes and hit the record button again.

"What happened last night Trenice?" Jordan asked.

"We'll find out soon enough – Jim what time is Chandler due in?" Roy asked.

"He's due in 4pm this afternoon." Get him on the phone immediately – we need him to cover your shift..."

"What the..."

"Jim, don't make me…"

"Yes sir! He said sarcastically as he got Chandler on the phone…

"Man I don't know what the fuck is goin' on – all I know is you gotta come in and cover my shift… yea he's here – you wanna talk to him?"

"I'll speak to Chandler later – right now I need him to get his ass in here," Roy said.

"You heard that right? I dunno man – you comin? Ok – I'll tell him…"

"He on is way Jim?"

"Yea – he's on his way – he'll be here in about 10 minutes…"

"Good – when he get's here I want you to bring those tapes from last night and meet me in the main office with Trenice and Jordan. – Trenice, Jordan – come with me."

"Ok Roy," Jordan said as we followed him to the main lobby and into the main office.

"What's going on Trenice?"

"Jordan, it's best for you to wait until Jim brings the tapes from last night then we'll all see what's going on," Roy said. I could see Jordan was about to explode so I had to come up with something quick…

"Roy, since you were nice enough to come back after your shift was over why don't you let me buy you some coffee?"

"I can get coffee from the cafeteria Trenice…"

"Roy, the coffee from McDonalds is much better than the coffee in the cafeteria…"

"That's ok Trenice – we can get coffee from the cafeteria…" Jordan is looking back and forth between the two of us wondering what the hell is going on…

"ROY, I'D LIKE SOME COFFEE FROM MCDONALDS – WOULD YOU PLEASE GO GET ME A LARGE COFFEE AND GET A CUP FOR YOURSELF?" It took him a minute to get the hint but he finally got it...

"Ohhh... ok – but since you're treatin' how 'bout some money?" he laughed.

"Here," Jordan said as he handed him a $5 bill."

"God – I thought he'd never get it," I laughed.

"What's going on Trenice?"

"Something happened last night Jordan," I whispered with tears in my eyes..."

"I know Trenice – I was here..."

"No you don't..."

"Oh my God Trenice – what happened?"

"He...he...he..."

"Who? Who Trenice?" Roy came in with Jim. Jim was holding the tapes under his arm.

"Here's your coffee Trenice."

"Thanks Roy."

"Jim, hand me those tapes," Roy said as he turned on the system and popped in the 1st tape.

"Not that one," I said. "We need to look at all of them," Roy said. "We can fast forward until we get to what we need to see."

"Ok," I said as Jordan and Jim look at us and at each other.

"That's Ceila – she's a regular," I laughed.

"Ok we'll fast forward this..."

"Wait! Who the fuck is that?" I yelled.

"That's Dr. Aiden," Roy said. "Why?"

"That's him," I whispered as I started to cry.

"Ok – you can go now – we'll take it from here," Roy said.

"Like hell you will," Jordan said.

"Sir – let us do our job – you're lucky you're in here," Roy said.

"Guess again," Jordan said. "You're lucky you're in here – if it wasn't for Trenice, Jim would have recorded over these tapes – so you're the lucky one."

"Aiight man – my bad – you right…"

"Yo – what the fuck? You see this shit?" Jim said as we all turned to look at the tape with Dr. Aiden in the room with me.

"I'll fuckin' kill him!" Jordan yelled as he punched wall.

"I had a feeling Dr. Aiden was up to something but I didn't have any proof – that's why I came back when Jim said it was you Trenice," Roy said.

"I'm glad you did," I said.

"Now I know why you went so crazy earlier – sorry Roy – I didn't mean to be insubordinate…"

"Don't worry about it – just make sure you hang on to these tapes…"

"How did you know what he did to you Trenice?" Jordan asked.

"Yea – how **DID** you know what he did to you?" Roy asked.

"I saw him do it."

"You saw him do it?!" they all asked in unison.

"Yea. If you didn't come in when you did he… he… he…"

"Thank God I came in when I did – I can't believe you actually saw him do this to you – I thought you were unconscious…"

"I was…"

"I'm not even gonna ask," Jim said.

"Well we know she's not crazy – we got the sick ass on tape!" Roy yelled.

"I'ma bust that muthafucka's ass when I see him," Jordan said.

"You can't do that," Roy said.

"Why the fuck not?" Jordan yelled.

"How would we explain it?"

"I don't give a fuck how you explain it – I'ma bust that muthafucka's ass!"

"Jordan you can't do that!" I yelled.

"Trenice I don't give a damn what you or anyone else says – I made you a promise…"

"Jordan you're not thinking…" Roy said.

"Roy, right about now I'm not tryin' to hear you or anybody else…"

"Honey please calm down…" I said.

"Trenice what's wrong with you? Don't you want him to pay for what he did to you?"

"He will honey – but you need to calm down and listen…"

"Ok Trenice – If that's what you want…"

"That's what I want…"

"I don't believe this fuckin' shit!" he yelled as he punched the wall…"

"They won't fuckin' believe this shit either…"

"She's right Jordan…" Roy said.

"How the fuck… what the fuck…" Jim said…

"Everybody listen!" Roy yelled. "First of all, we review these tapes every so often anyway – so let's just say for arguments sake – we reviewed these tapes and we saw what happened…"

"Ok – so why can't I bust his ass then?"

"Well for starters, technically, you wouldn't be in here with us when we review the tapes – so, technically, we would have handled this ourselves without you even knowing what went down."

"So basically what you're saying is you would have covered this up if it wasn't for Trenice?"

"No – I'm just saying we would have handled it – we would have dealt with the doctor and the hospital would be able to save face – you go bust his ass, he presses charges against you, you press charges against the hospital – the hospital brings me and Jim up on charges 'cause you not even supposed to be in here reviewing these tapes..."

"I don't fuckin' believe this shit! We gotta keep quiet 'cause you tryin' to protect the hospital? Fuck you and this hospital!" Jordan yelled.

"Honey please calm down..." I said.

"Trenice I'm not letting them get away with this shit..." Jordan said.

"I'm not either honey – that's why we're here – but they could both lose their jobs once the hospital finds out they let us review the tapes with them – we're not even supposed to be in here..." I reminded him.

"Fuckin' politics... can't get away from it... aiight – I'll leave it alone for now..." Jordan said.

"I know it's fucked up – but the only way we could do this and save our jobs is to tell them Trenice saw what happened – and we have no proof of that," Roy said.

"Yea it is fucked up – technically you should be able to sue the hospital and get paid but then we ass out if you do," Jim said.

"I wish there was some way we could get his ass and the hospital without involving you two," Jordan said.

"I have an idea," I said.

"Oh boy..." Jordan said.

"I'm afraid to ask," Jim said.

"Why don't you let us handle it from here Trenice?" Roy asked.

"Because Jordan is right," I said.

"See – that's what I'm talkin' about," Jordan said.

"What you gonna do Trenice? We have enough evidence to fire him as it is – shit I need my job!"

"I know Roy – but he needs to go to jail and Jim is right – technically I should be able to file a lawsuit against the hospital and get paid," I said.

"So what did you have in mind?" Roy said.

"Well, he's a doctor right?"

"Yea."

"So, doctors are required to take out insurance right?"

"Yea!"

"So we set the muthafucka up!"

"How we do that?" Jim asked.

"Well, if he did this to me, he's probably done this to other patients, and he's probably been doing it for a long time - right now he thinks he got away with it, so we need to be careful..."

"You right Trenice – but how do we set him up?" Roy asked.

"We need a room that doesn't have security cameras..."

"Shit – the only rooms we have that don't have cameras are the bathrooms outside the waiting area," Roy said.

"So we get him in the men's room outside the waiting area then I follow him into the men's room," I laughed.

"Trenice that's too obvious," Jordan said.

"No it isn't."

"What are you up to Trenice?" Roy asked.

"Simple. You take this ½ cup of coffee and you 'accidentally' run into Dr. Aiden. You get him to go into the men's room outside the waiting area. I go into the men's room, by mistake of course, thinking it's the women's room. Once Dr. Aiden comes into the men's room to clean the spilled coffee off his clothes, I make sure I come out the stall with my pants open, putting him in a compromising position. I scream, you and Roy come running, and 'catch' him in the act," I said.

"Damn that's some fucked up shit," Jim laughed.

"Not as fucked up as what he did to her," Roy said.

"I'm not sure I like this Trenice – what if it doesn't work? It'll be your word against his," Jordan said.

"Honey, that's only for the time being. Once I start cryin' and carryin' on, they'll review the tapes from last night – they'll think he's trying to pick up where he left off," I said.

"Then he loses his job and his pension – and he goes to jail too," Jim laughed.

"Just what the muthafucka deserves," Roy said.

"I threaten to sue the hospital, the hospital in turn sues him, he gets fired, they offer me a settlement out of court, which I am more than willing to accept," I said.

"Of course," Jim and Roy laughed.

"I still don't like it Trenice – I still wanna bust that muthafucka's ass," Jordan said.

"Oh you will honey – don't worry..."

"Trenice, you've been tellin' me this whole time to calm down – then you said I can't do that..."

"You'll get your chance honey..."

"When Trenice? How can I get a crack at his ass in Jail?"

"He'll be released on bail... then you just bide your time..."

"Damn – should I be hearing this?" Jim asked.

"You wanna get the muthafucka right?" Roy asked.

"Hell yea!"

"Alright then – shit – there's Dr. Aiden now... give me that damn coffee..."

"Roy wait!" I yelled.

"For what Trenice?"

"Le'me 'accidentally' go in the men's room by mistake first," I said as I jumped up and ran out the main office into the men's room.

"Whew – I really gotta pee," I said as I snatched my pants down and squatted over the toilet.

"Shit – stupid ass – I don't know why the hell he can't watch where the fuck he's goin' – old ass needs to fuckin' retire," I heard Dr. Aiden say as he came into the bathroom and turned on the water at the sink...

"Shit – you scared the shit outta me doctor," I said as I intentionally came out of the stall with my pants open.

"You know you're in the men's room Trenice?"

"Am I? Opps – I had to go so bad I didn't realize I came in the men's room," I lied. "Hey – how'd you know my name anyway?" I asked as I tucked my shirt inside my jeans.

"I had to fix your IV last night and I read your name on your chart," he said as he smiled at me mischievously.

"Son of a Bitch!" I screamed as I kneed him in the groin."

"Aaaggg.!" He screamed as Jim, Roy, and Jordan kicked open the door.

"What the fuck is goin' on in here? What are you doing in here with her doctor?" Roy yelled.

"That son of a bitch tried to touch me when I came out of the bathroom," I screamed.

"She's lyin' – I didn't even know she was in here!" he yelled.

"Is there a problem here?" The officer said as he came down the hall.

"Yes there is officer – this doctor tried to touch me when I came out of the bathroom!" I screamed again.

"She's lyin' – I didn't even know she was in the bathroom – I just went in there to try and get this coffee off my clothes 'cause this blind ass didn't watch where the fuck he was goin'!"

"I got your blind ass mutha fucka!" Roy yelled.

"What happened maam?" The officer asked me.

"I had to pee so I went to the bathroom."

"Why were you in the men's room?"

"Yea – why were you in the men's room Trenice?" Dr. Aiden sneered.

"I'ma 'bout 2 seconds off yo' ass!" Jordan yelled

"Sir who are you?"

"That's my husband!" I yelled.

"Oh ok – go ahead maam – what happened?"

"I was here last night – I went to go sign my discharge papers and I had to go to the bathroom so I told my husband to wait here – I ran into the bathroom 'cause I had to pee so bad – I didn't realize I was in the men's room..."

"Yea right – lyin' bitch..." Dr. Aiden said.

"I got your bitch right here," Jordan said as he lunged for Dr. Aiden...

"That's it – you're under arrest," the 2nd officer said as he grabbed Jordan's arms and threw his hands behind his back...

"Let him go!" I screamed.

"Let him go - we need to get to the bottom of this," the 1st officer said.

"Alright I'll let him go – but if you try that again you'll be leaving in handcuffs!" the 2nd officer said to Jordan. "Go ahead maam."

"So I'm peeing and I hear the doctor talkin' 'bout his old ass need to fuckin' retire – that's when I came out the bathroom stall..."

"Yea – why'd you have your pants open bitch?" Dr. Aiden said.

There was no stopping him. Dr. Aiden was on the floor and Jordan was standing over him wiping blood from his fist.

"Officer did you see that? I wanna press charges! I want his ass arrested!" Dr. Aiden yelled.

"No one's gettin' arrested until we get to the bottom of this!" the 1st officer said.

"Didn't you just see him hit me?" Dr. Aiden yelled.

"To be perfectly honest – I heard you call his wife a bitch – then I turned around and saw you on the floor – so to answer your question – no – I didn't actually see him hit you... go ahead maam."

"Well, as I said I came out of the stall and told the doctor he scared me."

"Did you have your pants open?"

"Yes."

"See? I told you!" Dr. Aiden yelled.

"Will you shut the hell up dammit!" the 2nd officer yelled.

"I had my pants open because I was fixing my clothes."

"What happened then?"

"He asked me did I know I was in the men's room and I told him I was in such a hurry to pee I didn't even realize it... he even called me by my name."

"What do you mean he called you by your name?"

"He knows my name.... ask him."

"Is this true?"

"Yes – she came in here last night – I told her I had to fix her IV and I remembered her name from reading her chart..."

"That's when he tried to touch me so I kneed him in the groin!" I yelled.

"Ya know something? That's the same shit you told me last night when I came in the room to see if she was ready," Roy said.

"Doctor, once you saw her come out of the stall why didn't you leave the bathroom? Why did you stay in there and attempt to carry on a conversation with her?"

"What? You actually believe this shit?"

"You wanna press charges maam?"

"Hell yea!" I yelled.

"Dr. Aiden you're under arrest," the 2nd officer said as he cuffed him.

"Get the fuck off me – you fuckin' bitch – this isn't over!" he yelled as they took him out the main entrance and shoved him into the car.

"You're right – by the time I'm finished with you I'll have your house and your pension – bastard!" I yelled as they took him away.

"You alright Trenice?" Jordan asked as he held me.

"No I'm not," I said as I started to cry. When he said he remembered my name because he had to fix my IV...and he grinned at me with that mischievous grin....everything he did to me came flooding back..."

"I remember him saying that to me too last night – he told me he had to take your gown off because they twisted the IV around your leg..."

"Sir we need to ask you a few questions," the 2nd officer said to Roy.

"Ok – shoot."

"You said he told you that last night? What did you mean?"

"Well, I didn't think anything of it at the time..."

"Go on..."

"Well as he said, she was in here last night for alcohol poising, and she was unconscious when she came in."

"How did she wind up with Dr. Aiden?"

"He was on call last night in the E.R."

"Oh ok – go ahead."

"So we had a victim from a car accident come in and I went to exam room #3 to see if she was ready to be moved into suicide watch."

"Why did she need to be put on suicide watch?"

"When she came in, her husband gave us an empty bottle of Tylenol and and empty bottle of Bacardi."

"Did she ingest the Tylenol?"

"No I didn't." I said.

"Maam I was talkin' to him."

"And I was talkin' to you – I didn't try to kill myself and I didn't take any damn Tylenol!" I yelled.

"Maam I'll get your statement after I'm done speaking with him ok?"

Jordan and I just rolled our eyes as he continued...

"Ok – what happened after that?"

"When I went to exam room #3 the curtain was drawn so I opened the door to ask if she was ready."

"Is that normal procedure?"

"It can be."

"What do you mean by that?"

"Well, as I said, the curtain was drawn so I opened the door and asked if she was ready."

"What happened then?"

"He said she was just about ready, but he needed to fix her IV because whoever put it in had it wrapped between her legs – I figured that's why the sheet was down to her knees and she didn't have her gown on when I opened the door."

"The sheet was down to her knees? And she wasn't wearing a hospital gown? She was completely nude?"

"Yes."

"Is that normal procedure?"

"Well, he said he had to remove the gown to take the IV from between her legs and put it in again – like I said – I didn't think anything of it at the time."

"What happened after that?"

"I came back to the booth and waited a few minutes more and she still wasn't here so I went back again to ask if she was ready 'cause we needed the room for the victim of the car accident."

"Was she ready then?"

"Yea she was ready."

"So did he take her to suicide watch?"

"No I took her – they needed Dr. Aiden to assist with the victim of the car accident."

"Did Trenice stay here all night?"

"Yes she did."

"Was anyone in the room with her?"

"I was," Jordan said.

"You have surveillance tapes from last night?"

"Yes," Roy said.

"Good – we'll need to take a look at those – I also want to take a look at the surveillance tape from this corridor if you have one."

"Ok – Jim, these officers need to take the surveillance tapes from last night and they want the one from this corridor."

"Ok Roy – I'm on it – you need Chandler to stay?"

"Yes – for the time being."

"Officers, come this way," Roy said as he led the officers into the main office and Jim went back to the booth.

"What do you think they're doing in there Trenice?" Jordan asked.

"I think they're reviewing the tapes."

"I hope they get that bastard."

"They will – but they might get you too."

"Don't worry about me – I can take care of myself – besides, if they see me knockin' the shit outta him and they arrest me I'll just ask them to put me in the same cell with his ass so I can finish what I started," Jordan said.

"Trenice?"

"Yes officer?"

"You're free to go now – we'll call you if we need you."

"Thank you officer."

"Shit – I wasn't aware we weren't free to leave in the 1st place," Jordan said.

"Well let's get the fuck outta here before something else happens," I said.

"I can't believe all the shit we've been through in the last 24 hours," Jordan said.

"Thank God Aunt Trudy wasn't here – all hell would've broken lose – especially with everyone else here." I said.

"You think your Aunt Trudy will find out?"

"Of course she will – They'll probably pass the tape around the staff," I sighed.

"I doubt that."

"What makes you so sure?"

"The officer's took the tape with them – no one will have it to copy."

"God I hope you're right," I said as we went to exit the hospital.

"Whatchu doin' here?" Char asked as she was walking into the hospital.

"Hi Char," we said in unison.

"Y'all alright?"

"No," I said.

"What's wrong Trenice?"

"I need my best friend," I said as she pulled me into a hug and I started to cry on her shoulder. Char didn't say anything. She just let me cry.

When I stopped crying she said, "Y'all goin' home?"

"Yea, were goin' home Char," Jordan said.

"I'm goin' wichall," She said as we started walking towards home.

"Char you ok?" I asked.

"Yea – why?"

"You were at the hospital..."

"Oh I'm ok – I came here to get my results."

"Results?" we both said in unison.

"Yea – remember you said I should get tested again?"

"Yea?" I asked.

"Well I did."

"Oh God... Noooooooooo!" I screamed.

"Trenice! Trenice!" Char yelled as I collapsed in Jordan's arms. "I'm ok Trenice – I'm ok!" she yelled as she shook me.

"You sure?"

"Yes!"

"So why were you here then?"

"I wanted to be here in case the results were positive."

"I should'a been there with you Char…"

"It's ok Trenice – I wanted to be alone."

"You scared the hell outta me just then – I thought we were dead."

"We? Ok that's it – what happened Trenice? And don't act like you don't know what the fuck I'm talkin' about either!"

"I can't talk about it now Char."

"Why?"

"There's too much to tell you."

"Ok I'll wait until we get upstairs – but I'm not leaving until you tell me everything."

"What if I don't want you to leave Char? Will you stay?"

"Depends on what you tell me Trenice."

Excerpt from:

How Far Are You Willing To Go?
(Rated PG) – Part 3

"You're not telling me what I want to hear," Jordan said.

"You don't understand," Detective Barros said.

"I understand perfectly," Jordan said. "You're the one who doesn't understand. He put his hands on my wife – now you have another problem – and you need to take care of it... before I do," Jordan said.

"I can't do that," Detective Barros said.

"You can take care of him just like you took care of what happened in the parking lot," Jordan said.

"You don't have to threaten me," Detective Barros said. "I get it."

"Glad to hear it," Jordan said. Detective Barros walked away from Jordan, got in his car, and drove off.